NECTAR

Ramona Drottoveo, an albino with unusual looks, is a chambermaid at a lush Italian country estate. Distinguished by an intoxicating scent, Ramona is despised by all women and worshipped by all men, whose inexhaustible lust she eagerly satisfies. But Ramona's life changes forever when she marries a sweet beekeeper who dies after discovering his bridge with a new lover on their wedding day. The superstitious villagers blame Ramona when his body mysteriously disappears and exile the couple from the estate. The story follows Ramona's tragicomic misadventures in the neighbouring city of Naples, where her life is transformed once again by the birth of an unwanted daughter, Blandina.

NECTAR

Lily Prior

**CHIVERS PRESS
BATH**

First published 2002
by
Black Swan
This Large Print edition published by
Chivers Press
by arrangement with
Transworld Publishers Ltd
2003

ISBN 0 7540 1887 3

British Library Cataloguing in Publication Data available

FOR CHRISTOPHER

I would like to thank Jean, as always, and Julia.

Chris, for your endless encouragement and enthusiasm, thank you. This is your book.

Thanks to every one who helped and heartened. *Nectar* needed you.

CONTENTS

CHARACTERS

In the Country

Ramona Drottoveo, the albino
The Signora, owner of the estate, and her
  husband, the Signor
Ovidio Gondulfo, the head gardener
Stiliano Mamiliano, the pig keeper
Ludovico Mamiliano, Stiliano's younger
  brother
Filippo Mamiliano, the boys' father, the
  retired pig keeper
Padre Jacopo Basolo, the parish priest
The old doctor, Blocco
Alfonsina, Dr Blocco's wife (later marries Dr
  Stipa)
The new doctor, Stipa
The beekeeper (the first of three)
San Ambrose, patron saint of beekeepers
Pupolo Floscio, the pastry cook's assistant
Trofimo Barile, the innkeeper at the Black
  Toad
Isolda Barile, Trofimo's wife
Dalinda Scandone, the kitchen maid
Sant'Ursula, invoked against plague
Immacolata Pescatore, the head cook
Ernesto Conticello, the rose gardener
Camilla Conticello, wife of the rose gardener
Roberto Pedretti, potboy, lover of Dalinda

San Gregorio, patron saint of music
San Cristoforo, patron saint of journeys
Selma Venerosa, the cheese-maker's one-eyed assistant
The lady Margherita, the Signor's married sister
Contessa Magina, a wedding guest
The lady Lydia, the Signor's third cousin once removed
Aunt Crispina, the Signor's aunt, dies during the wedding
The Duc'd'Alba, the Signor's oldest friend
The first Signora's brother at Roccamonfina
The lady Donatella, wife of the above, known as the Beast of Roccamonfina
Nuccio Pandolfo, the third beekeeper
Belinda Filippucci, Ramona's personal maid
Sebaldo Metrofano, son of Immacolata and Semprebene Metrofano
Casto and Polo, twin sons of Immacolata and Semprebene Metrofano
Maurilio Bergonzoni, son of the cowman
Silvestro Barbalace, Trofimo Barile's brother-in-law at Sparanise
Perseo, a young man who reeks of onions
Basilio Barile, son of Trofimo and Isolda Barile
Tullio, the Signor's prize hunter
Gordio Rossi, Gianluca Fuga, Lamberto Pedretti, all suitors of Blandina
San Andrea Corsini, invoked against sudden death

xiii

In the City

Nonna Pino, the shrine keeper
San Gennaro, patron saint of Napoli
Amanda Castorelli, landlord
Rupinello, the humpback
Santa Casilda, invoked for good luck
Amalasunta Castorelli, Amando Castorelli's wife, daughter of Nonna Pino
Signor Procopio Pastini, an admirer of Ramona
A dowager, patron of the Fontana
Modesta, companion of the dowager
Quintilla, Signor Pastini's cook
Policarpo Tebaldi, owner of the rag shop in the Via Acquaviva
Brunella Tosti, the whore who lives above Policarpo's shop
Giambattista Po, the artistic director of the opera house
Fanzago and Bottiglieri, Signor Po's enemies at the opera house
Panfilo, the caretaker at the opera house
The Seven Sleepers of Ephesus, invoked against insomnia
Padre Buonconte, the priest at the Chiesa di Santa Maria del Fede
Santa Maria Margherita, oversees the rite of exorcism
Rambaldo Melandri, the crib-maker
Everardo Donadio, the ringmaster at the Donadio Brothers Circus

Nabore, Valdo and Oddo, the injured man's sons

Blandina Buffi, Ramona and Rinaldo's child

Signor Scarpetta, a neighbour in the Via Vecchio Poggioreale

Selmo Filangieri, the owner of the Filangieri cook shop

Monalda Spantigati, the bearded lady

The Great Massimo, the strong man at the circus

Bubbone, Signor Pastini's butler

Liberio Borrelli, the butcher, one of Amalasunta Castorelli's suitors

PROLOGUE

At dawn, before the town of Aversa awoke from its slumbers, a sugar pink woman with white hair was observed by the gargoyles sneaking towards the portal of the convent of Santa Maria della Pieta. She was holding by the hand a tiny replica of herself, a girl aged about three, who was biting and wailing and dragging her little feet in the dust so that it rose around them in a cloud. The two disappeared into the vestibule and seconds later the woman reappeared alone, closing the heavy door firmly behind her, and hurrying away. She did not look back.

Part One

IN THE COUNTRY

CHAPTER ONE

THE GARDEN

Ramona Drottoveo was one of the chambermaids up at La Casa, the white marble palace in the valley of the Volturno, on the vast estate that had been in the Signora's family since the time of the Etruscans.

As Ramona worked 'indoors' rather than 'outdoors', and 'upstairs' rather than 'downstairs', she considered herself somewhat more important than the other workers on the estate. She began to look down on those who tilled the land, labouring in the lemon groves, the vineyards and the orchards, raising crops of sunflowers, chilli peppers, tomatoes, olives, and big-bellied melons; and she disdained those who tended the buffaloes and other livestock and those who worked in the dairy and the stables.

Ramona now thought herself above those who beautified the Signora's magical gardens, where peacocks strutted and fountains played orchestral music, where rare orchids bloomed, roses blushed, and where the lushest lawns stretched into the blue distance as far as the eye could see.

She even put on airs before those who roasted hogs, stuffed thrushes, sculpted ice, kneaded bread, plucked ducks, prepared pastries and polished silver plate and crystal goblets in the great vaulted kitchens.

Ramona was universally hated by the women, though not for this reason; being uppity was the least offensive of her sins. That which made women hate her, made men worship her; and this made the women hate her most.

Yet they weren't jealous of her looks, for she was ugly. Had Ramona been a beauty, they would have found the adoration she inspired less obscene, and far more tolerable.

The truth was, Ramona was an albino. Her plump body was bereft of all pigment. Her hair was as white as the feathers of the doves in the Signora's ornamental dovecote, and she refused to braid it, wearing it always loose in a halo around her face and shoulders.

Her skin was a violent shade of pink, so coloured by the blood flowing through it, and her livid moon face formed an ugly contrast with the white shade of her hair. Ramona's eyelashes were long and white, leading some of the female staff to compare them to those of the pigs in the pens beyond the vegetable gardens. Her eyes, where most of the colour in her body was concentrated, were also pink, like the eyes of the white rabbit you see in magic shows and picture books.

Yet, although she was coarse and candy-striped, the men of the estate flocked to

Ramona, and vied with one another for her favours. The women accused her of being a witch and of using evil arts to lure their men away; but Ramona was no witch. She simply had that scent about her that made a man in her presence forget the whole of his past life and seek to reinvent himself as a dog, if at that particular moment she wanted a dog. Or a cherry, or a new bonnet, or a visit to the circus. Work could be lost, opportunities discarded, wives and babes could go hungry, poverty and death could be biting at his heels, but still he would kick them up in the air and risk it all for one whiff of Ramona's elixir.

This is really what made the women hate her.

During daylight hours, especially in summer time, Ramona would not emerge from La Casa, for the world was too bright a place for her to inhabit by day. In the evening, however, she walked in the gardens, in the manner of the Signora herself, taking the air, and singing softly to herself the local folk songs, for she fancied she had a voice and loved to sing.

The Signora knew of this nightly intrusion into her gardens, and sought to put Ramona in her place, but on the advice of her husband, who was then enjoying the benefits of a regular coupling with the upstart maid, the Signora said nothing.

And so Ramona strolled with the peacocks through the walkways where the grass was manicured by a dedicated team of twenty under-gardeners. It was as green as crunchy apples and so springy it still bore the trace of her footprints long after she had passed by. Indeed it is said that Ovidio Gondulfo, the head gardener himself, was once seen prostrate in the acacia walk licking the imprints lovingly with his tongue after Ramona had left him for the bed of another man.

Then, when the scent hung plump in the air, and the wistful tenderness of the declining light made the garden the most romantic place on earth, Ramona would be accosted by countless admirers hiding in the topiary, imploring her to take pity on them and satisfy the agonized longing of their loins.

They came, not only from the estate, but also from the surrounding hills and sometimes even beyond. From the plains to the northeast and the west, and from the towns of Dragoni, Teano, Carinola and Mondragone. The admirers came from all walks of life, and it is fair to say that as word of her charms spread and her popularity increased, Ramona grew cold towards the field labourers with whom, in the early days, she had been content to satisfy her urges in the hayricks and beneath the hedgerows.

'What, Stiliano Mamiliano, are you here again? Do you think I will do it with you after the last time? Why the acorn that you feed to your pigs is a bigger prize than that which hangs between your legs.'

Deflated, Stiliano's head disappeared into the foliage, only to be replaced by that of his younger brother, Ludovico, fresh-faced and blushing.

'Will you do it with me Ramona Drottoveo?' he asked in a hoarse voice. 'My thing is much bigger than Stiliano's.' A thump followed as Stiliano's boot met the seat of Ludovico's trousers behind the hedge.

'I've no time for boys,' replied Ramona. 'I need a man who knows what's what.'

'Then take me, Ramona, please, I beg you,' came the voice of Papa Mamiliano, his head framed by lilac blossoms. 'I know what it takes to please a woman. Just give me the chance.'

'Take your two stupid boys and go home to your stupid wife, Filippo Mamiliano. And do it quickly before I lose my temper.'

Ramona marched ahead, her nose in the air which was drenched with her scent so that even the waters of the tinkling fountains were flavoured by it.

A little further along the walk, in the arbour of Venus, the parish priest, Padre Jacopo, was lurking behind the marble statue of the goddess, waiting for Ramona to appear. There was a time when Ramona had welcomed the Padre's attentions. But now that she could afford to pick and choose she was not so sure. What did the grizzle-haired priest have to offer her, anyway? Only his garlic breath and

9

shrunken member.

'Ramona, Ramona. Bend over I implore you and let down your drawers. Just imagine your upturned bottom with my magnificent manhood thrusting in and out of it.'

'Favour someone else with your magnificent manhood, Padre,' she replied, 'I'm not interested.'

Ramona, as the saying goes, had bigger fish to fry. The doctor had been at La Casa today, tending to her ladyship, who had taken to her bed with some imagined ailment. Ramona noticed she made a favourable impression on him when she carried a mustard footbath into the Signora's chamber, and hoped he would be waiting for her somewhere in the gardens.

Sure enough, as she walked through the beds of creamy lilies, she caught a glimpse of the doctor. He was skulking by the great sundial at the far end of the garden of the hours, hoping he was not visible from the house. He was sucking on a pipe and the smoke hung in a blue trail along the walk.

'Good evening, Doctor,' said Ramona in a low voice.

He jumped, already feeling the guilt that was to mar his life. As he turned to face her, something inside him heaved. He fell to his knees and embraced her skirts. His sobs broke loudly. His yearning was so strong it had turned him inside out. He knew he was ruined.

He would lose his wife and five children, his flourishing practice, his friends, his fine house in Santa Maria la Fossa. And yet he could not hold back.

Lifting the hem of Ramona's skirts, he kissed her stout boots, sobbing all the while, and then kissed her dirty stockings, all the way up her legs. Ramona was not accustomed to such preliminaries. None of her many lovers had ever bothered with any more than simply shoving it in and thrashing it about. She really quite liked this.

All around, hidden in sculpted bushes, rare trees, and exotic flowerbeds, the eyes of some of her previous and future lovers were watching in astonishment. What was the doctor doing to Ramona Drottoveo? Ramona glanced around, knowing they were there, enjoying her moment of glory.

Pulling Ramona down onto the grass beside him, the doctor slipped seamlessly inside her, and coaxing himself to a climax the like of which he had never known, with a cry he released his seed into her.

When it was over, the doctor rolled off onto the grass, shaking. He knew then that his life was over. Never would there be another moment to match this one.

He helped Ramona to her feet, adjusted his trousers, and kissed her lightly on the forehead before picking up his bag and going on his way. He did not look back. As Ramona shook out her skirts and retraced her steps to La Casa she had all but forgotten the doctor who was to take his life for her.

CHAPTER TWO

THE BEEKEEPER

Of the hundreds of men on the estate, or who were connected with it in some way, there was only one who never took the slightest heed of Ramona. She could walk right past him and he did not turn his head, or draw slowly, lovingly, into his nostrils her irresistible aroma. This irked Ramona, for she noticed such things, and she was determined that he too should fall under her spell.

This man was the beekeeper.

Tall and lean, he lived alone in a little cottage on the far side of the apple orchard. Here, in peace, he tended his hives, producing honey for the Signora's table, the medicinal royal jelly, and the beeswax used to polish the precious antiques.

The beekeeper was not a sociable man. He did not spend his spare hours drinking at the village inn with the other men. He preferred to spend his time alone. After a solitary supper, he occupied himself with his treatise on apiculture. He made drawings and notations in

12

a thick ledger. It was rumoured he was writing a book.

This did not endear the beekeeper to the local community, most of whom could not read, and who held a deep distrust of book learning. In the minds of the estate workers, scholarship was only a short step away from witchcraft. As a result they avoided the beekeeper as much as possible, hoping that this would keep mutant births, bad harvests, and the dreaded plague at bay.

Yet Ramona Drottoveo was not put off by such fears, and was determined to have the beekeeper join the other men of the estate at her feet.

Casual meetings did not seem easy to contrive, for when Ramona was at large in the gardens, the beekeeper was shut up in his cottage. She had only seen him a few times, largely at dawn when she had been hurrying back to La Casa after a night spent in rutting with the under-gardeners, fleeing the fast-coming daylight. It was on those occasions that he had had the impudence not to notice her.

Only that morning she had run quite naked through the orchard as the beekeeper struggled to remove a hungry mouse from a hive where it had spent the night munching the honeycomb. Even then he did not see her. Ramona boiled with fury.

'Who is he not to notice me?' she asked

herself later as she made up the Signora's bed, pounding the feather pillows as though beating the blind beekeeper.

'Stupid, stupid beekeeper.'

Dispensing with all thoughts of subtlety, Ramona decided simply to pay a call to the beekeeper at his cottage, seduce him, and forget him. As soon as the light had gone down, she emerged from La Casa. Already a line had formed outside the kitchen door.

'Ramona, Ramona,' began the plaintive cries of the desperate men.

As she passed by, trailing her magic scent in the air like fairy dust, embarrassing bulges formed in the trousers of the waiting suitors.

'You can all go away,' she called over her shoulder. 'Tonight, all night, I will be spending with the beekeeper.'

'The beekeeper!' said fifty astonished voices all at once. Suddenly a shower of hot water splashed over the crowd. The head cook, Immacolata Pescatore, had thrown a basin of dirty dishwater, achieving a fairly even coverage.

'Get away from my kitchen steps you dirty pack of dogs. I won't have this going on near my kitchen. It will curdle the milk. Get away from here, do you hear me? Dalinda Scandone, fetch me another basin. Quickly, girl, quickly.'

At this the dripping crowd dispersed, most of them following Ramona along the path that led to the orchard. Dalinda Scandone was too late with the second basin and received a slap to her face for her tardiness.

'Immacolata Pescatore, why do men follow Ramona Drottoveo everywhere she goes?' asked Dalinda, still smarting from the slap.

Immacolata Pescatore added another slap for discouragement: 'You don't need to know such things, Dalinda,' she said. 'We'll have none of that talk in my kitchen.'

Meanwhile Ramona and her retinue had reached the beekeeper's cottage.

'Aren't you afraid of the plague, Ramona?' asked Ernesto Conticello, the rose gardener, elbowing his way to the front of the throng.

'I'd rather catch plague from him than greenfly from you,' Ramona remarked as she knocked loudly on the door.

As the door opened Ramona forced her way inside and closed it behind her. The beekeeper, whose mouth hung slightly open and whose eyes had grown round, was clearly astonished. Women did not usually force their way into his cottage. But he said nothing and waited for an explanation.

Ramona treated him to one of her smouldering looks. The silence between them was taut. Ramona knew in a single instant that he felt her power and was struggling to resist it. He was caught in her web just as surely as were all the others.

'Do you know who I am?' she asked

imperiously.

'You are Ramona,' he replied in a dry-mouthed whisper. 'Everybody knows you.'

'And so why do you not look at me when I am near?'

'I cannot.'

'Why not?'

'I do not allow myself to.'

'And did you not look at me this forenoon, when I passed by you, naked?'

'Then most of all I could not allow myself to look.'

Now it was Ramona's turn to be astonished. She had never before encountered a man with self-control.

'And why do you not allow yourself to look at me?' she asked him.

'Because I could not bear to look upon you and not possess you,' he answered earnestly, 'and therefore I do not allow myself to look.'

'And now that you are looking at me, do you want me?'

'Yes.'

'How much?'

'More than any of those men out there,' he answered, gesturing with contempt towards those who were surrounding the cottage, climbing the apple trees, breaking the branches, and peering in at every casement in search of a better vantage point.

'I desire you more than my own life, and that's the truth.'

16

'Then you shall have me, right now,' said Ramona, satisfied with his answer, and she began to unfasten the buttons of her gown.

'No,' cried the beekeeper in anguish, turning away from her and grasping his head between his hands as though in pain. Under his breath he murmured a quick prayer to San Ambrose, the patron saint of beekeepers, for strength in the face of temptation, then he said: 'I don't want it to be like that, the way it is with all the others. I've seen you with them. I know what goes on . . .'

'Then what do you want?' asked Ramona, puzzled.

'I want it to be as it is in my imagination, as I see it in my dreams . . .'

'And how is that, beekeeper?'

'I want to court you. I want to walk with you in the summer meadows, holding your hand; I want to hear the song of the nightingale with you. I want to weave daisies into your white hair; I want to recite to you my poetry: all the poems I have written about you, and all those I have yet to write; I want to tell you everything that is in my heart. I want to give you my love and win yours; then I will kiss you tenderly and ask you to be mine for ever, to be my wife.'

Ramona was flabbergasted: never, not even in the farces performed at festivals by the wandering players, had she heard a speech of such perfect nonsense.

'All right, beekeeper, I'll marry you,' said

17

Ramona, removing her long drawers.

The crowd outside began to jeer at the sight of Ramona's bare pink thighs.

'No,' cried the beekeeper, thumping his forehead against the wall in his agony and frustration. 'San Ambrose, I beg you, give me strength. It cannot be like this. I haven't asked you to marry me yet. Please, I beg you, let it be as I have dreamed.'

'You really don't want to fuck?' she asked incredulously.

'Ramona, sweet, sweet Ramona: how sweet your very name sounds upon my lips. I have never allowed myself to say it aloud before. I would not be a mortal man if I did not desire to make love to you immediately. But it cannot be like this: not with this circus outside, not until we really know one another, not until you love me as I love you, not until we are married. Allow me to call for you tomorrow evening at dusk. We will start by walking out together.'

He bowed to her and opened the door. She was still in a state of shock. So shocked in fact that she forgot to put on her drawers and left the cottage without them. After he had closed the door behind her the beekeeper noticed them and picked them up from the floor where they had fallen. Their bewitching scent, Ramona's scent, filled the room. The beekeeper inhaled it and wept.

CHAPTER THREE

THE COURTSHIP

Ramona crossed the orchard like a sleepwalker. Her interchange with the beekeeper had the surreal quality of a dream. She was barely aware of the presence of the crowd still following her. Their voices seemed to bubble through water, reaching her in strange distortions of tone and volume. She walked through the gardens in the same manner and finally reached La Casa. Saying nothing she went inside and closed the kitchen door behind her.

The crowd bore the look of sceptics who had just witnessed a miracle. The majority pressed on to the Black Toad in the village to seek an explanation from Trofimo Barile, the innkeeper, who was widely acknowledged to be a man of the world, and at the same time to drain a few draughts of his wife's excellent ale.

Others remained behind, convinced that Ramona would re-emerge from the house, and, smarting from the beekeeper's rejection, would seek solace in the arms of the first man she should chance upon. The eighteen left in the courtyard sized one another up with sneering looks, each of them determined to be that man.

19

Back in her little room, high up in the eaves of La Casa, Ramona lay on her bed thinking. Should she marry the beekeeper and begin a new life? She rather thought she would. She was so bored with her situation, at the advanced age of nineteen, that she was ready to do almost anything that would bring about a change, even a change for the worse.

Marriage with the beekeeper would have its advantages: for one thing, as a married woman she would no longer have to work for the Signora. How tired she was of the endless carrying of mustard footbaths, making beds, plumping pillows. '*Si*, Signora, *no*, Signora.' Bowing and scraping, pandering to her every whim.

Oh if only she could leave this life behind and begin again somewhere else. How she dreamed of the city lights which lay to the south. If only she could leave the estate for Napoli: for there, she knew, she would be completely happy.

A tap on the door interrupted her musings. It was the Signor, wearing nothing but his riding boots, and carrying a cane. Ramona giggled with delight as she jumped up and threw her legs around him and with a cry of 'Tally ho!' he impaled her upon his outstretched member.

The following evening, true to his word, the beekeeper, wearing his Sunday best, came to call at the kitchen door for his sweetheart.

20

Dalinda Scandone, who opened the door, immediately brandished the crucifix which hung from her girdle to ward off any plague vapours that the beekeeper might exude into the air. 0040707017

'Sant'Ursula protect me,' she cried. 'Protect your daughter Dalinda Scandone. Let me not succumb to the plague, Holy Mother, and I promise to wash my feet and my ears and not to let Roberto Pedretti touch my intimate parts and I promise to . . .'

'What's that, girl?' interrupted Ugo Rossi, the under-butler overhearing her prayers. 'I'll have to tell Immacolata Pescatore that you've been allowing Roberto Pedretti to touch your intimate parts. It's not sanitary in a kitchen, for one thing.'

'No!' screamed Dalinda Scandone. 'Ugo Rossi, I beg you, I beg you not to tell her.'

'It's my duty to let her know the depravity of her kitchen maids. It's for your own good, Dalinda.'

'No. No. No!' screamed Dalinda, terrified, her cheeks already smarting in anticipation of the slaps they would be forced to bear.

'Excuse me,' interceded the beekeeper, who was by nature a patient man, but there are limits to everyone's patience. 'If I might just say something?'

Dalinda screamed and raised the crucifix once more. 'Sant'Ursula protect me from the pustules,' she bellowed.

21

'Dalinda Scandone, calm yourself, please,' said the beekeeper, exasperated at last.

'But you brought the honey on Thursday,' said Dalinda Scandone in obvious confusion, waving the crucifix in his face.

'Yes I did. This time I have not come to bring honey.' He spoke his words carefully so the slow-witted girl would understand him.

'Oh,' she said, preparing to close the door on him, reasoning that if he had not come to bring the honey, he could go away again.

The voice of Ugo Rossi could still be heard in the background, taunting the witless maid.

The beekeeper put his arm out to hold the door saying: 'Dalinda, please tell Ramona Drottoveo that I am here.'

'Ramona Drottoveo?'

'Yes, Ramona Drottoveo.'

Dalinda Scandone began to bray at the top of her voice: 'Ramona Drottoveo, Ramona Drottoveo, Ramona Drottoveo.'

All the noise brought Immacolata Pescatore herself to the door. She quickly administered a slap to the cheek of Dalinda Scandone: it was the only way to silence her.

'Now beekeeper, what is it that you want?' asked Immacolata in a businesslike manner.

'Please would you tell Ramona Drottoveo that I have come to call for her.'

'Not you as well, beekeeper?' Immacolata Pescatore asked with obvious disapproval. 'I thought of all men, you would have more sense

22

than to involve yourself with that, that . . .' she struggled to find a word that was sufficiently damning but still ladylike: she failed. 'That baggage,' she spat out at last.

'Please, Immacolata Pescatore, do me the favour of not speaking of Signorina Drottoveo in that way. All I ask is that you let her know I am here.'

Immacolata Pescatore drew herself up to her full height, which, in truth, was not very high, and bowing with hauteur she retreated into her kitchens, directing the silver maid, Beata Viola, to seek out Ramona.

Some time later, when Ramona felt she had kept the beekeeper waiting a sufficiently long time, she appeared at the door.

The beekeeper bowed and offered her his arm, and sought to conduct her towards the lower pastures, which were quite achingly beautiful at this time of year.

Several of the footmen idling in the yard followed behind, and gradually others fell in with their number: the blacksmiths, the grooms, the carriage drivers, the under-gardeners, the chimney sweeps, the pig keepers, the cowmen, the buffalo-milkers, the ploughmen, until the crowd was, if anything, larger than on the previous evening.

Undeterred, the beekeeper pressed on, pointing out to Ramona the various items of natural interest and beauty that they came across upon the way. Gently he drew her

23

notice to the kingfisher skimming the stream; the nest of baby voles; the amazing toadstools; the wild orchids which he gathered and wove into her hair; the swallows; the stars as they came out. Ramona feigned a slight interest, which the poor beekeeper seized with the gratitude of an enthusiastic puppy.

'Ramona, dear, sweet, Ramona. I feel so close to you,' he said in a voice rich with emotion.

In the darkness the beekeeper did not notice Ramona's yawns, and he interpreted her sighs as signs of love rather than of boredom. As he led her and her pack of followers back to La Casa, he promised to call for her again the next evening, and this time, to read her some of his poetry. At the door he took the liberty of planting a chaste kiss upon her forehead, and placing his hand in a romantic gesture upon his heart he made his way home to his little cottage.

That night the beekeeper was unable to sleep. He tossed and turned in his bed until he became entangled with the sheets and had to kick at them violently with his legs to free himself. His every thought was of Ramona. Her scent filled his nostrils still. It hung in the very air around him. It stirred up his blood. It maddened him. He could see her face before him in a rosy vision. He loved the turn of her cheeks, her pink blinking eyes, her cloud-like hair. Physically he loved everything

24

about her and his elastic member responded like a jack-in-the-box to every delicious thought.

It would be wrong however to presume that the beekeeper's attraction to Ramona was based solely on her physical charms. He fantasized that there was a spiritual understanding between them, the like of which had never been experienced between a man and a woman in the entire history of the world. As they were so compatible, so well suited to a harmonious life together, the beekeeper determined to accelerate his plans and bring forward his proposal.

Ramona too was unable to sleep that night, but not for thoughts of the beekeeper. She had admitted herself into the footmen's dormitory, and as an act of revenge for such a monotonous evening, was making a clockwise circuit of the twenty-four beds which lined the walls.

CHAPTER FOUR

POETRY

'Ramona, sweet Ramona, colour of the ocean's pearl,' began the beekeeper in a dramatic tone.

It was the evening devoted to poetry, and

the beekeeper had installed Ramona on a rug on the banks of the stream while he stood, lantern in hand, reading aloud from a notebook.

There were eighteen sonnets, eleven odes, some verses of mixed length and three epigrams all on the theme of Ramona. In addition he had invented a new free-style form of poetry especially for her; this would allow him to express the true depth of his feelings without the constraint of composing in rhyme. The poetry made the onlookers laugh as they huddled together at a little distance listening intently, but the beekeeper read on without taking the slightest notice of their loud guffaws. Ramona did not laugh: for the most part she was snoozing on the blanket after the exertions of the night before.

'Well, Ramona, that is the last,' he said finally, closing the book. 'Although I could always run back to the cottage and get the next volume if you wish it?'

When he received no reply, the beekeeper swung around the lantern to discover Ramona's sleeping form nestling on the blanket. Far from being annoyed, he was touched by what he regarded as her complete trust in him, and he crept towards her and began stroking her hair.

'Sweet, sweet little thing,' he murmured. 'She's tired. I have been boring her with my reading. Ramona has no need for poetry: she

26

is poetry itself.'

He gathered her up in his arms, careful not to wake her, and carried her tenderly back to the house, where he gave her up into the less tender care of Immacolata Pescatore. He knew that the next day he would ask Ramona to be his wife.

He did, and she accepted him, and by the end of the week the beekeeper found himself in the Chiesa di San Stefano, marrying the girl of his dreams in a ceremony conducted by his bride's former lover, the priest, Padre Jacopo.

Spectators squashed into the pews of the dusty church, and Stiliano Mamiliano, who arrived late, was forced to sit on Ludovico's lap throughout the service. Even later arrivals like the two peacock keepers, the troupe of acrobats who just happened to be passing, and the blind beggar who, having been lured by Ramona's scent, had taken a wrong turning, were obliged to stand at the back.

Every man was crying for his loss. Even Padre Jacopo was sobbing fast as he conducted the service, his tears falling like silver beads on the front of his surplice. How many of them pledged themselves to eternal goodness; to stop drinking; to attend mass twice on Sundays, and every day during the week; to stop gambling, whoring, cursing, fighting, and, in the case of Padre Jacopo, to stop dressing secretly in women's clothing, if only the marriage could be prevented. But it was not to be, and three hundred and eleven hearts were broken as Ramona made her pledge to the beekeeper. The dusty floor of the *chiesa* was washed by tears.

They returned to the cottage as man and wife, in a little pony and cart lent by the Signora. She blessed the marriage, and hoped that as a married woman Ramona would mend her ways.

The beekeeper was by now mad with desire for Ramona, who was exuding the magic fragrance more flagrantly today than she ever had before. The pain in his groin was growing more and more urgent, and his member was so confused by the conflict between its own feelings and the attempts of the beekeeper to keep it down, that there was very nearly a tragedy with every jolt of the cart.

The bride, Ramona, was already planning her adulterous encounters: the Signor was insistent that she come to him in the Library that very night, and she was amusing herself with the thought of the outrageous lies she would be required to tell her new husband to account for her absence.

'At last my wife, we are alone,' murmured the beekeeper as he led her inside the darkened cottage. He carried Ramona into his bedchamber which he had prepared with rose petals and honeysuckle and lavender. He had also taken the precaution of closing the shutters to prevent the unwanted attention of

28

his rivals who were now applying their eyeballs to the cracks in the wood.

As the beekeeper lost his virginity behind a veil of spangled stars, his wife lay back with a glazed expression on her face; she had not even noticed the consummation of her marriage, and did not attempt to suppress her sighs of boredom mixed with resentment. The beekeeper slipped gently into a comatose state of bliss; she left the marriage bed for the assignation with her lover.

'And so, Mistress Bee,' said the Signor moments later as he rode Ramona on all fours around the Library: 'How is the married state?'

'I think I shall die of boredom,' she replied pitifully.

'Poor little filly,' said the Signor, bringing his whip down with a thwap on her pink buttocks, 'I am sure we will be able to supply a little diversion to prevent such an awful fate. Gee up, old girl,' he shouted loudly with another crack of the whip.

Much later that evening Ramona crawled back into the bed of her husband, her bottom covered in red weals. The movement of the mattress roused the beekeeper from his delicious semen-scented slumber.

'Ah my darling,' he murmured thickly, 'I thought I had dreamed you, but no here you are, as real as anything. I have been remiss to fall asleep. Why, I haven't even given you your wedding gift yet.' He clambered out of bed and lit the lamp.

'Why, my angel,' he cried in consternation, catching sight of her livid bottom amongst the snowy white sheets, 'how did you get those horrid marks on your beautiful posteriors? Surely I did not do that to you?'

Ramona nodded her head, her eyes glittering with the lie.

'Oh my poor sweetheart,' he cried piteously, falling to his knees by the side of the bed and kissing the wounds, 'will you ever forgive me?'

Ramona said nothing, wisely assessing that her husband's guilt was the currency that would buy her many freedoms.

Finally, after a thousand kisses had expiated the beekeeper's guilt, he presented her with his wedding gift: a lumpy parcel wrapped in paper and tied up with bows. She removed the paper to discover a pair of bulbous eyeglasses. The lenses were as thick as the width of her finger and were encased in a rubberized mask with an adjustable head-strap.

'What are these things?' she asked, turning them around in her hands and examining them closely with her weak pink eyes.

'They are eyeglasses, my love. When you wear them you will be able to go outside in daylight, for the special glass will filter out the sun's strongest rays. Try them on.'

Ramona adjusted them over her nose, and pulled the strap over her head. For the first time, she was able to look directly at the lamp without squinting. Her thoughts flew with wings towards the delights that now lay in store for her. She could hardly wait for the dawn so she could test them out in daylight and see how much more fun she could have.

CHAPTER FIVE

THE EYEGLASSES

The following day found Ramona out amongst the dolphin topiaries in the full glare of the sun. How wonderful it was to be released from her monotonous duties in the Signora's chamber! She had begun to think that marrying the beekeeper had been worth it for the eyeglasses alone. Admittedly they did look rather strange, but Ramona thought them beautiful. She paraded herself in front of the other women tauntingly. They regarded this development with dismay. Up to now their husbands had only been liable to temptation after working hours: how many men would now lose their jobs for daytime dereliction of their duties?

It took some time for Ramona to grow accustomed to the eyeglasses, for the thick lenses, while they reduced the glare, also made everything seem further away. It was disorientating, and she had slipped and fallen down more than once. As she landed on her face in the dewy grass for the third time her eyes came level with a pair of boots. She looked up and saw that the owner of the boots, in themselves a perfectly ordinary pair of boots, was the most godlike creature she had ever seen. Immediately and unequivocally and for the first and last time in her life Ramona Drottoveo fell in love.

'Signora, may I assist you?' spoke a voice that plucked a secret string.

She allowed herself to be assisted. Once on her feet she examined the owner of the boots and the voice at close quarters. He was tall and broad shouldered with a mane of copper-coloured curls which hung in clusters like grapes around his head. The stranger's eyes were so dark as to be almost black; they were warm and velvety and fathomless. His nose was copied from a Roman statue. His mouth, which eased into a wide smile during this encounter, revealed fine white teeth.

The classic nose had not been slow in detecting Ramona's scent, and the man attached to it was already smitten.

'Who are you?' asked Ramona in wonder.

'I am Rinaldo Buffi,' answered the seductive voice. 'I am the new beekeeper's assistant.'

What a wonderful turn of fate!

'Then you must come with me,' said Ramona, winding him into her sticky web. 'I am Ramona, the beekeeper's wife.'

Shortly afterwards, in the muscular arms of the beekeeper's assistant, in the bed of the beekeeper, Ramona Drottoveo discovered the meaning of life.

As she roused from her stupor, the situation dawned upon her with the clarity of glass: here was the man she should have married. It had all been a huge mistake. With such a man she would be happy for the rest of her life: beyond that, for eternity.

'Rinaldo Buffi,' gasped Ramona, prodding him with a plump pink finger. 'You must kill my husband.'

'Yes, of course. Immediately. Anything,' he gasped back from somewhere far away, immersed in an acid bath of ecstasy that was busy dissolving him. 'Only tell me what to do, and I'll do it. Never let me be apart from you again, Ramona. Ever.' His head slumped back onto the beekeeper's pillow. He was only half alive.

At this juncture the door opened and the beekeeper entered the chamber.

It took some moments for him to understand what was happening. On hearing strange screams coming from his cottage, as he knelt by his hives in the orchard, he feared for the safety of his bride and came home at a run. But the screams were not, as he first thought, those of fear, such that Ramona would make if she was being attacked and robbed by gypsies, or if she was being stung by bees. No. They were rhythmic, and rose and fell like the waves of the ocean hitting the shore. They welled and ebbed, grew in volume and urgency and then became calmer. They seemed, if anything, almost like cries of joy, like bliss.

On throwing open the door to his bedchamber the beekeeper saw two figures in his bed. One was his bride, Ramona. The other appeared to be his new assistant, Rinaldo Buffi, to whom the steward, Semprebene Metrofano, had only recently introduced him. What was he to think? It could not be real. The beekeeper took in this scene with a slow glance and then turned around and left the chamber, closing the door behind him.

Even Ramona Drottoveo was momentarily discomposed. Rinaldo Buffi, who had opened his eyes at the opening of the door, was mortified. What had he done? Here he was, with the man's wife, in the man's own bed! He wanted to die of shame. What should he do now? Should he run? Escape by climbing through the casement, and just keep on running? Or should he stay and somehow fight it out? Could he bring himself to grapple with the beekeeper, and kill him as Ramona had instructed?

None of these proved necessary, for the beekeeper was already gone, leaving an empty space full of awkward thoughts and feelings.

'What shall we do?' asked Rinaldo in a

desperate voice, fearing the beekeeper would return with a loaded shotgun.

'Oh, don't worry about him,' said Ramona. 'He will do nothing, and later, if he returns, you will deal with him.' She had already seized hold of her lover and was inciting him to repeat his crimes against her husband.

'Yes, I will deal with him when he returns,' Rinaldo heard his own voice saying without reference to his will. Then, yelping, he submitted once more to his mistress's demands.

The beekeeper, meanwhile, finally grasped the horror of his situation. Walking through the orchard, slowly and deliberately he discarded his protective clothing: his gauntlets, his helmet with its thick veil of mesh, his apron and smock. Throwing them to the ground in his wake he made towards one of the hives, and with his bare hands removed the cover. A cloud of angry bees rose into the air at this intrusion. Within seconds the beekeeper had fallen to the ground clutching his throat; his extreme allergy to bee stings was known only to himself.

It was only later that Stiliano Mamiliano and his brother Ludovico came to the cottage with the news and the body on a makeshift stretcher. Ramona and her lover were still in the beekeeper's bed. The marriage had taken place barely twenty-four hours earlier, and already Ramona was a widow.

As the pig keeper and his brother deposited the corpse on the table in the little parlour, Ramona was already celebrating. Everything had happened to her satisfaction. Now she was free to enjoy the love of Rinaldo Buffi; for her no longer the boredom of the beekeeper. How wonderful life was once more.

Rinaldo, however, was less satisfied. The events of the last few hours did not seem real. It was like a dream. Or a nightmare. Everything was happening far too fast. His life had started spinning out of control. He wanted to slow things down. Stop for a moment to think, but there was no time. He was being swept along by a force much greater than his own feeble strength. He was powerless to resist it.

With the corpse stiffening on the table Ramona silenced Rinaldo's protests and drew him back into the bedchamber. Rinaldo's conscience struggled valiantly but lost the battle. His only escape from the awful conflict of guilt and desire was to submerge himself so deeply in Ramona's essence that everything outside of her ceased to exist. Oh what a night they then enjoyed, a night of a thousand nights.

CHAPTER SIX

A SINISTER DISAPPEARANCE

The next morning, when Ramona went into the kitchen to brew some coffee, the corpse was missing from the table in the parlour. It had simply gone. Vanished.

'Rinaldo, come and look,' called Ramona in amazement. 'The body has gone.'

Rinaldo stumbled in. She was right. The body had gone. Surely it was the work of the devil. Rinaldo quickly crossed himself. How could a corpse simply disappear? The copper-coloured hairs on his shoulders stood up on end.

'I don't like this, Ramona,' he said. 'I don't like this at all. There is something evil going on.'

'There's nothing evil,' said Ramona dismissively, kissing him deeply. 'Don't you see how the fates are smiling upon us, Rinaldo? I want the beekeeper to die, to leave us free to be together. I decide you must kill him. Just as I decide this, he is found dead, by a miracle, through no act of ours. It is an act of God. He is struck down for being in our way, for seeking to come between us. It is ordained. We are meant to be together. His body is placed on the table in the parlour. We make love

37

again and again and again throughout the night. When we rise we discover the body is gone. Good. I don't like to have his body around the place. Everything is happening just as Ramona likes it. Don't be fearful. Be joyous. Our union is blessed by the Holy Mother herself.'

When Semprebene Metrofano heard about the disappearance of the body he felt a chill in his heart. Bad luck was sure to follow such an unnatural event. Immediately he organized a search of the entire estate. He gathered together a band of men, and together they prayed to San Antonio, who helps those who seek something they have lost. Following the prayers, the men rubbed the soles of their boots with the leaves of the horseradish plant. According to local folklore this would prevent them from walking into danger.

Then Semprebene Metrofano dispatched the men in twos and threes to the pigpens, the cowsheds, the haylofts, the stores, the barns, ditches, hayricks, stables, even the Signor's wine cellars and the attics of the great house, and all the places where Ramona had conducted her affairs in the days before her marriage. No trace of the beekeeper could be found. Not so much as a whisker. San Antonio was biding his time.

The steward tried in vain to keep the news from the Signora, fearing the probable consequences. But the hue and cry was such that she found out and took immediately to her bed with a smelling bottle, a crucifix, and the necklet of dried olive pips that had always brought her luck. She feared death more each day, and any mention of it brought on one of her attacks.

To appease his wife the Signor even offered a reward of fifty scudi for the safe return of the corpse. This gesture of largesse resulted in various corpses being brought in, some of which had, no doubt, been recently exhumed for the purpose. Unfortunately none of them could be successfully identified as the beekeeper.

The villagers were quick to predict disaster. There would be famine for sure and, likely as not, flood, eruptions of the distant volcano, storms, cyclones, plagues and freak births. The estate had not forgotten how Floriana Redenta, wife of the then miller, had given birth to a black piglet all those years ago; pregnant women wailed and called down curses upon Ramona while pleading in the same breath with Santa Margherita for intercession and a natural birth.

Trofimo Barile, during this period of fear and uncertainty, made enough money to buy a new wagon and even had enough left over for some trimmings to enliven the bar. He returned from a trip to Capua with a brass lamp and a looking glass with a gilt frame in which his wife Isolda regarded herself with a look of satisfaction each time she had cause to pass by. Trade had never been so good, nor was it to be again, for Trofimo was moving ten barrels of ale every day.

Yet it was not just his wife's excellent ale which brought the workers from the estate to the inn, jostling one another to find enough space to raise their cups to their lips; Trofimo Barile's unique form of wisdom was what the community most required at that time. The priest, Padre Jacopo, was still chasing after Ramona and was of no help to anyone. Some of the more religious women on the estate even considered approaching the Bishop with a complaint about Padre Jacopo, but as so often happens in such situations, no-one, in fact, did anything. In this climate of spiritual and moral fear, Trofimo Barile became the man of the moment.

On the night of the disappearance of the corpse, the crowded bar, assuming a respectful silence, listened as Trofimo recounted a story he once heard while working as a cellar hand at the White Horse, far to the north in the town of Urbino.

A local dignitary, Signor Raymondo Barbuzzi, had died of the jaundice after a protracted period of illness, and in accordance with tradition the yellow and bloated body had been laid out in the front parlour to receive the visits of family, friends and government officials.

40

Within the space of five minutes, between one civic councillor leaving the parlour and partaking of some light refreshments, a little Marsala and a number of the Widow Barbuzzi's celebrated almond *biscotti* in the morning room, yes, during this brief interlude and the entry of his Honour the Mayor of the nearby town of Fossombrone, the body simply vanished.

This singular event led the Widow Barbuzzi to lose her mind and she was interred with the criminally insane in the vaults of the San Paolo Monastery which had been turned into an asylum after the death of the last of the *fratelli*.

An exhaustive search was carried out which stretched across the region from Rimini in the north to Gubbio in the south, and east and west to similar distances. No-one, and Trofimo Barile stressed this point, no-one had seen so much as a flap of yellow skin, or a strand of matted hair which would indicate that the body had passed that way. No sign of Signor Barbuzzi was ever found. The body had vanished without trace from the surface of the earth.

'Now, if you ask me what I think,' continued Trofimo, as he polished a tankard carefully with a cloth, 'I don't think Signor Barbuzzi was ever really dead at all.'

The drinkers shuddered. What was anyone to think? All this was too confusing for the mind to contemplate. Another round of ale was ordered and the gruesome conversation about the undead and disappearing bodies went on late into the night.

Although, in life, the beekeeper had not been popular, in death he assumed the cachet of a martyr. The workers insisted they had always loved him. Some pretended they had named their children after him or had invited him to celebrate feast days with them. Some claimed to have gone hunting with him in the woods, or to have played him at chess. Trofimo Barile took the opportunity of placing a plaque in his honour on the front wall of the inn, although far from being a regular patron of the Black Toad, the beekeeper had never once gone in there.

Even though the search for the body had proved fruitless, within the week a funeral was arranged. A lightweight coffin was put together by Silvestro Bernini the carpenter, and a great many mourners gathered in the churchyard for the service. Among them was a woman, a stranger to the estate, tall and gaunt and thickly veiled. It was obvious from their physical resemblance that this was the beekeeper's mother.

A choir of matrons sang the Ave Maria, little children clutched crosses or stems of lilies, and Trofimo Barile gave such a touching eulogy of the man they all loved like a brother that the beekeeper's mother collapsed under the weight of her grief, and it was only the timely intervention of the pig men that prevented her from toppling into the gaping grave.

Ramona, to give her the limited credit she deserves, did not pretend to play the part of the grieving widow during the ceremony. Wearing the bulbous eyeglasses, the wedding gift of her dead husband, she frolicked openly with Rinaldo Buffi, coaxing and wheedling and playing with him until his gasps of pleasure mingled with the sobs of the mourners.

She and her lover did not attend the tea afterwards given, by the grace of the Signora, in the servants' hall of the great house. After the warm air swallowed up the final words of the benediction, they were seen running back to the beekeeper's cottage, already shamelessly shedding their clothes along the path through the orchard.

After the grave was filled with earth, the beekeeper's mother mingled with the crowd. She was touched to learn how they had all loved her son: from the humblest dairymaid, Virna Fuga, to the steward, Semprebene Metrofano himself. Later Trofimo Barile took her to the inn where she was shown the plaque raised in her son's name. She did not have the heart to point out to the innkeeper that her son was teetotal.

Afterwards Immacolata Pescatore provided a handsome spread in spite of the Signora's instructions that it was to cost no more than

43

three scudi. As Immacolata herself had said, it was the least they could do to give the poor beekeeper something of a send-off.

From the women the beekeeper's mother learned much about Ramona. She heard of her birth on the island of Capri; how she was abandoned by her mother, who was also an albino; and how she was brought up by the nuns in the convent of Santa Maria della Pieta in Aversa until the Signora took her into her service at the age of twelve.

They told her about Ramona's precocious sexual development; how she had seduced, wholesale, the men of the estate: husbands, sons, brothers, grandfathers, lovers; how no man was safe from her clutches, not even, it was rumoured, the Signor himself.

They told of their disbelief and horror when Ramona turned her weak yet greedy eyes on the one man on the estate who had long remained impervious to her evil charms. The man, who was now dead as a result, was the beekeeper.

Two weeks later, flouting public opinion and basic decency, Ramona and Rinaldo were married in the same little church in the village. Outside, the empty grave of the beekeeper was a black blot on the green grass of the churchyard. This time there were no onlookers from the estate, not a single one. For some reason the men, in a gesture of solidarity with the beekeeper, had stayed away. The

44

shambling sexton and his wife who infrequently brushed the church floor to redistribute the dirt acted as reluctant witnesses.

For the bride and groom, this was the happiest day of their lives. Rinaldo carried Ramona in his arms all the way back to the cottage and their lovemaking continued uninterrupted for three full days.

CHAPTER SEVEN

ILL LUCK

After the marriage Ramona and Rinaldo lived in bliss in the beekeeper's cottage in the apple orchard. To the surprise of many, and perhaps even to herself, Ramona remained faithful to her new husband. Women everywhere breathed sighs of relief.

Although men still followed her whenever she emerged from the cottage, begging her favours, Ramona was not even tempted. Even when the Signor sent his personal valet, the pompous Tito Livio Feriani, to summon her to the Library, still she did not succumb and sent back a coy message informing the Signor that her heart and other bodily parts now belonged to another. The Signor accepted her decision with equanimity, and besides, there was a new stable boy who was by then attracting his interest.

Yes, Ramona really had changed since her marriage to Rinaldo, and she knew in her heart that she would never want another man.

Life on the estate was also changed, although it was not for the better. Rumbles of discontent were everywhere: the workers, previously satisfied with their lot, were now wretched; their wives complained ceaselessly about everything and everybody. Lifelong friends became enemies; engagements were called off; fights broke out between neighbours, and even brothers; children cried and contracted colds and verrucas.

Not only the people but also the land and the animals were affected by the general disaffection. The harvests were poor: beetles infested the rye and a great column of ants chomped through the wheat fields. The sunflowers succumbed to a fungus. The melons exploded. A fire mysteriously consumed one of the vineyards. There was blight in the fruit trees and the nuts mouldered on their branches before they were ripe. Fervent prayers were offered up to San Ansovinus to protect the harvests, but he seemed to be ignoring them.

One of the prize sows tended with such care by Stiliano Mamiliano suffered a stillbirth and seventeen piglets were born dead. On the same day a dog went mad and frothed at the mouth, sending the entire estate running for safety until it was cornered and shot. A stampede of cattle in the lower pastures trampled the cowman Bernardino Bergonzoni, leaving him with a broken leg. The peacocks lost their magnificent tail-feathers and the doves flew away and were never seen again.

It was only a matter of time before the community connected this ill luck to the disappearance of the beekeeper's corpse.

One day some of the women met, by chance, outside the gamekeeper's cottage, and sat down to gossip on a grassy bank in the shade of the walnut tree that formed a canopy over the dusty lane. Like everybody else on the estate, they were preoccupied with their misfortune, and debated how they should appease the restless spirit of the beekeeper.

Bibiana Mamiliano, mother of the pig men, suggested a mass and the lighting of votive candles. Andromeda Doria, the gamekeeper's wife, thought this course of action insufficient, and was keen to hold a seance, for she prided herself on her supernatural powers. Saturnina Floscio, Pupolo's aunt, wanted to slaughter a black bullock and three red pullets at midnight, but the others balked at the idea of animal sacrifice, and secretly determined to report Saturnina to the Bishop. Gloriana Tomacelli, the weaver, was just expounding on her view that the only way to pacify the beekeeper was to punish Ramona, by whipping her publicly, or putting her in stocks, or both, when the widow-bride herself skipped into view.

'There she is, the cause of all the trouble,' cried Bibiana Mamiliano, pointing out Ramona to the indignant throng, as she rounded the bend in the lane.

'Whore,' shouted Gloriana Tomacelli.

'Hussy,' called Andromeda Doria.

'Murderess,' cried several voices all at once.

'Body snatcher!' shrieked Milvia Lucentini, the midwife, with venom.

'If it wasn't for her, none of this bad luck would have fallen upon us,' was the general consensus among the matriarchs.

All the women made the sign of the horns at Ramona, which roused her fury to such a pitch that she ran at them and assailed the whole company with bites and scratches and kicks. There was such a hullabaloo that Semprebene Metrofano and his band of men who were pruning in the arboretum heard the rumpus and advanced at a run.

Ramona had Gloriana Tomacelli face down in the dirt and was pounding her with her fists when Milvia Lucentini grabbed hold of Ramona's white hair and began tugging at it with all her strength. Ramona bit and kicked and indeed was in such a fury that in error she administered a nasty bite to Semprebene Metrofano as he sought to pull her away, leaving the lobe of his ear hanging by a thread.

48

'She's a wild animal, that's for sure,' said Bibiana Mamiliano while searching the ruins for her porcelain teeth that had become dislodged during the fracas. There were wisps of hair and torn pieces of clothing and shoes and other debris strewn all around. Even a wooden leg was discovered, although no-one claimed to have lost it.

Semprebene had lost so much blood that he had to be carried to the great kitchens to receive first aid from Immacolata Pescatore. The women left behind lost no time in circulating rumours that he had contracted rabies and soon Padre Jacopo appeared at La Casa preparing to read the unfortunate steward the last rites.

Meanwhile, Semprebene's men returned Ramona to the beekeeper's cottage. Holding her close to prevent her fists from flying caused much excitement amongst the band of men entrusted with her care. More hands than were strictly necessary to control her were applied to her person and they took the longest possible route to the orchard to prolong their proximity to this most captivating creature. In fact, once they arrived at the cottage after a journey of some two hours, Rinaldo was ready to challenge some of the group to a fight for what he regarded as improper behaviour towards his wife. However, Ramona, who had seen enough violence for one day, pulled Rinaldo inside,

49

dismissing the men with a snarl and some well-directed barbs relating to the manhood of one or two individuals.

Semprebene Metrofano, his ear heavily bandaged, could not avoid mentioning this latest incident to the Signora at their weekly meeting in which the garden and the other issues relating to the estate were discussed. The Signora took a dim view of things, and resolved in her mind to be free of the troublesome maid once and for all.

That night the Signora admitted her husband to her chamber for the first time in eleven years, and taking advantage of his surprise asked him to give Ramona and Rinaldo notice. Since the Signor was no longer able to ride Ramona around the Library and beat her with a whip, he thought it best to humour his wife, and agreed that the couple should go.

And so, the following day, Ramona and Rinaldo were asked to leave the garden paradise where their love had burst open like an autumn flood, sweeping them away in its irrepressible tide.

Rinaldo loved living on the estate. True, in the snatches of sleep Ramona allowed him at night, he was tormented by terrible dreams, recurring nightmares in which he was slowly stung to death by a suffocating swarm of giant bees all with Ramona's face. But in his waking hours he was deliriously happy, and reluctant to leave.

Ramona, for her part, was furious at being dismissed in such an ignominious manner. Yet soon she came to regard the dismissal as a golden opportunity. She had long dreamed of exploiting her singing talent. Now the idea came to her like a visitation: she would make the journey to Napoli and become an opera singer, a great diva, the new Tetrazzini. She knew, despite everything people said, she had a wonderful voice. Given the right encouragement she would become a star.

In bed that night Ramona outlined her plans to Rinaldo. She would become the prima donna at the famous Teatro San Carlo, and he could find well-paid work of some kind, she was sure. Everybody on the estate knew life was easy in the city, and it was full of amusements. Together they would enjoy the theatres, the circus, the fancy shops, the festivals and the carnivals. Yes, there would be excitement at every turn.

Rinaldo, whose life with Ramona provided as much excitement as any man could handle, knew it was useless to argue with her. He held to himself the view that his wife would make a more competent grape-picker than an opera singer. He had not the heart to tell her that her singing voice sounded like a cracked pot struck with a stick. Despite his doubts, Rinaldo could not bear to disappoint his bride, so he kept his reservations to himself. A day or so later, with their few belongings packed into a handcart, they left the magical gardens for good.

CHAPTER EIGHT

THE FESTIVAL

The villagers saw the lovers off on their journey with boos and jeers and hisses. Some of the women threw rotten fruit and vegetables at Ramona as she passed by. An over-ripe tomato burst against her back, showering her with seeds. Bruised aubergines buffeted her. Yet Ramona sallied past like a queen, pausing only to make an obscene gesture at those she hated the most.

After they had gone, and the tantalizing scent finally trailed off into the distance, there was much rejoicing, and a party was thrown in celebration. The church bells sang out the cheerful peals usually reserved for feast days and weddings. The Black Toad was bedecked with brightly coloured bunting in honour of the occasion, and rows of trestle tables had been set up in front for the feasting, sheltered from the heat of the sun by the shade of the great plane tree. Beyond, an area of the dusty square had been swept ready for the dancing, and some professional musicians were set to play late into the night.

Isolda Barile and her serving maid, the towering Pudenziana Esposito, had been up all night working tirelessly in the kitchen, and the spread they had put together truly was magnificent. An octopus of monstrous size had been brought specially all the way from Pineta Mare, and required three men to carry it. Nobody, not even Trofimo Barite, who had seen most things in his lifetime, had ever seen one so big. It was stewed whole over a fire in a massive cauldron filled with tomatoes, olive oil, peppers and garlic. The aroma it gave off was so intoxicating, it lured crowds down from the surrounding hills: shepherds, minstrels, bandits, even a column of leprous pilgrims walking barefoot to the shrine of San Floriano at Carditello. All thoughts of the pilgrimage were abandoned as they lined up with great wooden bowls alongside the buffalo-milkers and lemon-harvesters and the under-butlers from La Casa.

And that was just the beginning. Fresh pizzas kept emerging from the wood-burning stove, carried to the tables by a red-faced and roasting Pudenziana Esposito, whose brawny forearms were as thick as the trunk of the shady tree. Steaming and gooey, the pizzas were loaded with a rich cargo of mozzarella, tomatoes and basil. Stuffed with salty ricotta and home-cured salami, the folded pizzas were the best ever tasted in the region.

Wine and ale flowed as freely as the slow river snaking round behind the inn, and the faces of the feasting folk soon began to glow and glisten. There was a cheer as Pudenziana Esposito staggered into view under the weight of a suckling pig with all the trimmings, and a lucky dip was held for its tail, the most succulent morsel of the whole roast. When it was won by the witless kitchen maid Dalinda Scandone, she passed out with the excitement and required several sharp slaps from Immacolata Pescatore to rouse her.

Platters of figs drizzled with honey followed the main course, and then there were *sfogliatelle* pastries filled with curd cheese, candied oranges and cinnamon. Stomachs were groaning with all the good things inside them, and the sun was going down by the time the last morsels were swallowed. The host, Trofimo Barile, wearing a green velvet cap with a golden tassel, stood up to propose a toast:

'Neighbours,' he began. 'Nay, more than neighbours, friends, although it is true to say that a good neighbour is better than a friend, I ask you to join me and be upstanding . . .'

There was much scrabbling as the benches were pushed back and those with big bellies and wobbly legs and fuzzy heads attempted to stand. On one table, the stable boys and under-gardeners who had indulged a little too freely in the host's excellent ale went down like

54

dominoes, and fell laughing into the dust.

'May the departure from the estate of Ramona Drottoveo and Rinaldo Buffi put an end to the bad luck we have experienced here of late. I hereby call upon the spirit of the wronged beekeeper to leave us be and to pursue those two on the road to Napoli, for we are innocent folk and never meant him any harm. Friends, please raise your cups and drink with me to an end to the evils.'

'An end to the evils,' chorused one and all, and drained their cups to the dregs.

On cue the music began, and it was not long before the sozzled villagers, slumped once more along the benches, their buttons and buckles straining, were joining together in the melodramatic folk songs for which the region is justly famous. They swayed back and forth together in slurred versions of *Funiculi-funicula*, and *Torna a Surriento*, and when Stiliano Mamiliano who was blessed with a glorious baritone gave a heartfelt rendition of *O sole mio* there was not a dry eye on the whole of the estate. Propped up on pillows in her darkened chamber in La Casa, the Signora wept. Even Isolda Barile's mange-blighted cat Massimo blubbed inconsolably and his tears formed a milky pool in the dust.

After the singing came the dancing, for those who were still able to co-ordinate their movements. For the *Trescone* six of the footmen appeared in makeshift turbans, and pranced around Beata Viola who was got up as a sultana with diaphanous veils and a pair of giant pantaloons stolen from the washing line of Andromeda Doria.

The finale came as Immacolata Pescatore and Semprebene Metrofano performed together as the lovers in the *Tarantella*. What a handsome couple they made. With what fire did they gaze into one another's eyes at every dip and turn. They seemed lost to the world, immersed greedily in one another, and after a while the spectators began to feel like gooseberries, and so drifted away in twos and threes to the campfire where shadows were dancing, apples were roasting, and where Virna Fuga was telling fortunes.

The guitars, tambourines and castanets filled the night air with their song, and brought out the silver stars, one by one. As the melody washed over the villagers a feeling of calm benevolence descended upon them, the gift of Sant'Irina, beloved of peace, who, watching from on high, saw the estate was sorely in need of harmony. It was almost like old times before misery and despair had fallen upon them.

What a wonderful day it had been. They would still be talking about it for many years to come. There had never been a fête to match this one.

Sure enough, the beekeeper's curse was gone. His ghost was out on the road to Napoli, pursuing Ramona and Rinaldo.

Part Two

IN THE CITY

CHAPTER NINE

THE CITY, AT LAST!

Ramona sang softly to herself all along the route that led from the estate through Capua Vetere and down to Aversa. Wearing her eyeglasses, and carrying a cheap paper parasol to prevent the sun from burning her livid flesh, she gave her own unique renditions of *Mi chiamano Mimi* and *Teneste la promessa* which she had learned from the Signor. The beauty of her voice thrilled her, and she couldn't wait to begin her new career. Her only regret was that she had wasted so much time in the country, on that boring estate, among those crass and ignorant people.

Rinaldo, pushing the cart containing their baggage, was less happy. While Ramona's joy gave him pleasure, the weight of responsibility for their future lives rested heavily on him. Throughout the journey he was plagued by doubts and pestered by rogue bees. They buzzed around his head and bombarded his ears. He couldn't seem to shake them off.

Footsore after many hours of walking, Rinaldo and Ramona finally arrived in Napoli as the bells of the thousand churches were striking five haphazardly, and the great city was busily bustling back to life after the brief lull of the siesta. Between the towering marble *palazzi* of the *centro storico*, multitudes surged like a human ocean. Neither Ramona nor Rinaldo had ever seen so many people gathered in one place at the same time, and they were swept along, anchored to each other and to the handcart, while their eyes and ears soaked up the wonders of the city.

In this whirlpool of life, fine ladies paraded beneath parasols, wearing brightly coloured silks and feathered hats, some cradling miniature dogs that Ramona at first mistook for rats. Sharp-suited gentlemen conducted business in the shade of colonnades. Dandies in loud-patterned trousers gathered in groups, gossiping. Pigeons pecked for scraps, scurrying between the passing carriages and carts whose wheels swiftly pulverized the nuggets of horse manure into dust.

In the Via Tribunali schoolchildren in pinafores skipped along two by two. Nuns in blue habits clutching crosses hurried to mass. Mules brayed. A knife fight broke out between two dwarfs, and ended swiftly in their simultaneous deaths. A wedding party collided with a funeral cortège and the bride collapsed with grief at her ill luck. Packs of wild dogs ran amok barking and growling and baring their teeth.

Further on, a contingent of guards in green uniforms and plumed helmets escorted a manacled prisoner to the *carcere*. The Piazza

Miraglia was filled by a procession of bishops in purple robes on their way to San Domenico Maggiore. They were accompanied by barefoot friars ringing hand bells, choirboys in scarlet, and priests bearing a life-size plaster effigy of San Gennaro from which the paint was peeling. The rear of the procession was brought up by a blind man with a hurdy-gurdy, led by the hand by a chimpanzee wearing a sailor suit and carrying a cane.

In the Via San Sebastiano water carriers and lemonade sellers, bent double under the weight of their great terracotta flagons, bawled out advertisements for their wares. Ragmen peddled unsanitary scraps. Whores touted for business. Octopus vendors produced steaming *polpi* from boiling apparatus positioned on the pavement. Acrobats tumbled across the Piazza Gesù Nuovo. Fire-eaters swallowed flaming swords to the roars of the crowd. Shrivelled beggars scavenged. Pickpockets prowled, and a trio of hairy-faced women strummed mandolins and warbled folk songs.

Ramona's lips flapped with awe as she gawped at these new species. In her innocence every man seemed a prince, every woman a queen. She was so excited she felt giddy. Oh how she loved it here already. Napoli surely was a paradise.

Through no will of their own, they were carried along by the crowd into the Strada di Toledo, where trams trundled, their brakes

61

screeching and bells clanging. Here, of course, were the finest shops to be found in the whole of the city. Ramona peered closely through her eyeglasses at every grand window display, her nose clouding the glass with a vapour which she wiped away periodically with her grubby fingers. On display were beautiful shoes of the softest leathers, in rainbow colours. She would take every style in each colour. In fact, she would probably take two pairs of each, just in case she happened to spoil one pair by stepping in a mire.

Her attention was then drawn to the arts of the milliner. In the reflection of the plate glass Ramona regarded her own ugly cap with hatred. It was details such as this that separated her from the princesses around her.

She required a pretty bonnet without delay. But the choice was bewildering. How could she even begin to decide? Here were hats piled high with feathers; with jewelled pins and exotic flowers like those that grew in the Signora's garden; and others with alluring little veils through which she could imagine her pink eyes peeping seductively.

'Look, Rinaldo, don't stand there like an oaf with your hands in your pockets,' she said: 'look at these bonnets trimmed with ribbons and lace.'

Then there were the gowns, each of them more beautiful than anything she had ever seen, even in her dreams. Silks, brocades, satins and taffetas. Velvets encrusted with pearls, cashmere, gold and silver, scarlet, purple, pink and blue. These creations made even the Signora, the only fine lady Ramona had ever known, look like a peasant girl in homely attire.

Immediately Ramona's imagination was at work, picturing herself dressed in such finery, adorning the streets during the *passeggiata*. It would only be a matter of time, she convinced herself, before she would be making her glorious début at the opera, when the gentlemen would be reduced to tears by the beauty of her voice and would fall faint at the sight of her loveliness. She would hobnob with dukes and duchesses, counts and countesses, princes even. No longer would she make her way through the streets on foot with Rinaldo following behind with a handcart. She would have her own carriage, horses and footmen; and she would not sleep with the footmen, though they would be the most handsome footmen in the city.

Ramona was so absorbed she didn't hear anything Rinaldo said to her, and wandered like a sleepwalker between the wonderful shopfronts, making a mental list of the things she would return to buy prior to making her entrance into society. All Rinaldo could do was follow behind, and occasionally haul her out of the path of a passing carriage or cart as she vacillated between the opposing magnets of tempting goods on either side of the busy street.

After trudging behind Ramona for several hours Rinaldo thought it was time for them to proceed with more important matters, like finding lodgings. He saw how passing men were sniffing the air, filling their nostrils with the tantalizing molecules of Ramona's scent, and he didn't like the looks they were giving her. More than once Rinaldo had to threaten with his fist a cheeky barrow boy or sailor who loitered too close. He could see he would need to keep a watchful eye on Ramona in these streets teeming with villains. Vain and foolish as she was, any knave could charm her and mislead her. Already he had misgivings about the city. Should they really have come?

Ramona didn't see why they couldn't take an apartment right here amongst the shops. That way she wouldn't have to carry her purchases any distance to their lodgings. In due course she would naturally have a boy, perhaps a eunuch in livery, to carry her packages for her. But regardless, living any distance from the shops would be inconvenient.

At this even Rinaldo, patient man that he was, began to feel exasperated. Ramona seemed to lack any understanding of their situation, and he was concerned at the dizzy heights her expectations reached. She knew only too well what the Signora's severance terms were: one month's wages to help them get set up in the city. A beekeeper's wages were not high, and this small sum would barely support them until Rinaldo found work.

In the hurly-burly a face loomed towards him which reminded him of the beekeeper. For a second he thought it was him, and his heart stopped, but then he realized his mistake. Just a passing similarity, that was all.

CHAPTER TEN

THE HOUSE OF CASTORELLI

As Rinaldo predicted, finding lodgings was not an easy task, especially as nightfall was now approaching. He regretted allowing Ramona to waste the daylight hours in folly, staring in shop windows at things they would never be able to afford.

For hours they tramped around the shabby district of Villaria without success. Every place they tried Ramona violently disliked for one reason or another. One was too small and cramped, one was too dark, and one was up too many flights of stairs. Rinaldo was growing disheartened. He had not seen Ramona's fussy and demanding side during those idyllic days on the estate. Now they were in the city, she seemed to have changed. Rinaldo knew he had to take something or they would be spending the night on the streets.

Last to try was an address in the Via Vecchia Poggioreale. Here crumbling buildings struggled to hold themselves up, three-legged dogs and scabrous cats roamed in packs, and smut-spattered laundry hung from washing lines criss-crossing the narrow street. Ramona was quick to wrinkle up her nose in disgust.

Just outside the dingy doorway sat a moth-eaten woman, the shrine keeper, Nonna Pino. She had just lit the candles dedicated to San Gennaro, and was starting on her knitting.

'Good evening, signora,' said Rinaldo, placing a few coins in the *offerta*.

Nonna Pino looked at these strangers in alarm. First she scrutinized Rinaldo's face and then Ramona's. Whatever she saw there brought a shadow across her cloudy eyes and she crossed herself vehemently, repeatedly, and then grasped the little amulet of coral around her neck.

'It's ill luck that follows you,' she said. 'Misery, pain and death are at your heels. Don't you see them?' She pointed with a gnarled hand into the gathering darkness.

Rinaldo looked fearfully behind him but saw nothing, only Ramona's grimacing face.

'We've come about the rooms,' he said.

'San Gennaro protect us,' the crone muttered towards the shrine. 'Save us from the evil I smell in the air.'

'She's mad,' said Ramona. 'Let's go. It may be contagious.'

Just then a man appeared behind the bent figure of the shrine keeper. He pinched her crumpled cheeks trying to draw out a smile, and failing, pulled her cap down over her eyes for a joke.

'Death!' she cried, 'Son-in-law, 'tis death knocking at the door.'

The man exchanged a conspirator's glance with Rinaldo and beckoned the lovers inside. Together they climbed the stairs to the top floor apartment. Signor Castorelli, as he was later identified, was a fat and greasy man in his fifties with lard-like skin and the smell of a wet dog come in from the rain.

On the landing he stopped under the lamp and opened his mouth wide to show them he had no tongue. With his fingers he made a gesture in the air, as though drawing a plume of breath out of his mouth, and then he shook his head violently: he could not speak. The tongue, it transpired, had been lost some years before in a freakish accident, leaving him completely dumb.

The apartment looked even worse than even Rinaldo had anticipated. Signor Castorelli's hand signals indicated its limited attractions one by one. He stroked the grubby paper lining the walls, so faded you couldn't tell what colour it had once been. He appeared to conduct an orchestra before the rear windows, but all that could be seen was the abattoir and more dilapidated tenements beyond. The kitchen area was particularly depressing with its filthy sink which Signor Castorelli caressed, and chairs with uneven legs. In the other room, with nudges and winks to Rinaldo, Signor Castorelli leapt onto the fetid mattress of the bed and bounced up and down to demonstrate the strength of the springs.

Despite Ramona's tears, Rinaldo paid Signor Castorelli one of their few precious scudi for the first month's rent. How his eyes gleamed at the sight of the coin, which he tested between his teeth before tucking it lovingly into a pouch concealed in the toe of one of his boots.

Rinaldo then went to retrieve their few belongings from the handcart he had left at the entrance. Outside, Nonna Pino was still wailing: 'Plague. Death. Evil. He, the fool, opens the door and invites them into the house. Misery will come of it. Misery.'

Meanwhile, Signor Castorelli, whose nose was still fully functioning, had detected Ramona's scent in his nostrils, and was making obscene gestures to indicate the strength of his attraction to his new tenant. Ramona armed herself with one of the broken chairs and in a similar dumb show mimed what she intended to do with it, whereupon the signor beat a hasty retreat down the stairs to the safety of his own apartment.

Ramona sobbed and sulked at finding herself in such a dwelling. Where would she hang her beautiful clothes? Where would she keep her new bonnets and pretty shoes? When she asked Rinaldo these questions, he felt it best to humour her. She had suffered enough disappointment for one day.

'We won't stay here long, *bella*,' he told her. 'We'll move somewhere better, with a big wardrobe for your dresses and things. Just be a little bit patient, that's my sweet girl.'

This satisfied Ramona and she soon bounced back to her cheerful self. After all she was now in the city, the wonderful, beautiful, exciting city. That night she saw sweet dreams which featured princes and feather boas and satin slippers and banquets and circuses and handsome cavalry officers and she awoke the next day refreshed and happy and eager to visit her new clothes in the Strada di Toledo.

Rinaldo, however, experienced a restless night. At first he could not fall asleep with all the worry. Where would he find work? And what could he do? There was probably small demand for beekeepers in a place like this, and he had no experience of anything industrial or commercial.

Towards the morning, when he did finally fall asleep, he had a horrible dream. A noose was tightening around his neck, crushing his windpipe. His hands were tied behind his back

69

and his legs were swinging high up off the ground. There was a sack over his face. He began to gag. His breath was bursting his lungs. Blood began to fill his eyes, and he knew he was already dead.

CHAPTER ELEVEN

DISGRACE AT SPINELLI'S

Despite his reluctance to leave Ramona alone and at large in the city, Rinaldo planned to set out early to look for work. While they drank their coffee and ate their rolls, Ramona gave Rinaldo a little advice on the kind of work he was to take.

'I would like it best,' she said, 'if you became a cavalry officer in a blue uniform with striped trousers and a plumed helmet. But if not, a banker would be almost as good.'

In truth, she did not even know what a banker was, but the word sounded good.

'Or a civil servant, or an admiral or a merchant or an orchestra conductor. I wouldn't like it if you became a newspaper vendor or a doctor or a soap-maker.'

'I'll have to see what I can find, Ramona,' Rinaldo replied with patience. 'I can promise you, though, I won't become a doctor.'

As he left the apartment, a tiny man was

passing who had a pronounced hump on his back. Humpbacks were, of course, highly prized at that time for their magical powers. A stroke of a humpback's hump was known to bring good luck to the stroker. In the city humpbacks made a prosperous living by allowing their humps to be stroked, selling lottery tickets, and telling fortunes. What happy chance that there should be a humpback living right there in the very same building! Rinaldo, with his superstitious nature, was comforted by this good omen, and offered up a silent prayer to Santa Casilda, in thanks for this upturn in their fortune.

'*Salve*, neighbour,' said Rinaldo, already feeling luck tingling in the tips of his fingers.

'*Salve*,' replied the little man, noting Rinaldo's admiration for his hump. 'I am Rupinello. If you want to stroke my hump it will cost you five grains. My regular fee is a *carlino*, but as you are my neighbour, I offer you a discount.'

Needing no further prompting, Rinaldo fished a coin out of his pocket and gave it to Rupinello before stroking his lucky hump several times.

'Now you'll see, Ramona,' called Rinaldo up the stairwell. 'Today will be a good day, an auspicious day.'

The little man had lost no time in filling his nostrils with Ramona's scent, which was so potent early in the mornings. It hung heavy in

71

the air like a juicy cloud. He poked his head into the apartment to look at the creature emanating the fragrance.

'What a funny little man you are,' said Ramona, studying him through her eyeglasses.

'I may be funny,' replied Rupinello with dignity, 'but I can bring you good luck. I can interpret the numbers. I can help you to win the lotto.'

Ramona shrugged. She cared nothing for lotto and other forms of gambling.

'I can make your dreams come true,' he said, sensing her weakness.

'Can you?' she asked, her interest growing.

'Yes,' he said. 'And I can tell fortunes.'

'I do need my fortune told,' said Ramona, 'and I need help with my plans. They are not dreams indeed, for they are real things, not fancies, and are sure to happen anyway. But I would like it if you could make them happen very soon.'

'I am your man,' said Rupinello grandly with a bow. 'And I am at your service.'

'You can expect to hear from me then,' replied Ramona equally grandly as she closed the door on him. Reluctantly Rupinello pulled himself away from the aroma and set out for a day of strokings.

Ramona sat in front of the cracked looking glass on the washstand and gave herself along look over. She needed to decide which of the hats she had seen yesterday would suit her

72

best. She also considered the dresses, measuring their various merits until the velvets, satins and tulle became a whirl in her mind.

'I know,' she said to herself brightly, thinking of a clever way of clearing the confusion, 'I'll just take them all.'

Someone tapped on the door. Ramona reached for the big knife, fearing it was Signor Castorelli. She opened the door cautiously, but it was not the landlord. It was his wife, Amalasunta, daughter of Nonna Pino. A small woman with buck teeth and a weeping scar over one eye, she had acquired the habit of miming from her husband, although she was perfectly capable of speech.

'I like to go through the rules with the new tenants as soon as they arrive,' she said, waving her arms above her head, 'just so there are no misunderstandings.'

She rattled through the exhaustive list of rules. It appeared there was to be no singing or playing of musical instruments except during fixed hours. To illustrate the point she stood up and held her throat with a sublime expression on her face, and then imitated the playing of a violin. There was also to be no drunken behaviour and no dogs. Now she got down on the floor on her hands and knees and emulated the wagging of a tail with one of her arms held behind her. Ramona wanted to scream. What a madhouse! They really would

73

have to leave immediately.

'And don't mind Mother,' she said finally as she went out. 'She gets excited but she doesn't mean any harm. And make sure the rent is paid on the first day of the month, for I don't give credit.'

Ramona already felt a violent hatred towards the Castorellis. If she wanted to draw water outside the given hours or play a trombone at any time other than ten o'clock on Tuesdays, then she would, and let them do what they could about it. She would not be bossed around as though she was still in service. She had come a long way from the Signora's bedchamber. She took orders from no-one.

Bristling, Ramona resolved to leave the house as soon as she was ready and head towards the shopping district. Only the sight of the delights in the fancy shops could cheer her. She would not stay in these rooms another moment.

Outside Ramona encountered the shrine keeper who was squatting down taking a pee.

Nonna Pino began to bellow: 'Satan. Pink devil. Horns. See how the horns rise up from her head like white hair.'

'You're a disgusting old woman,' Ramona told her, picking her way daintily through the rivulets coursing towards her.

Before she had reached the end of the Via Vecchia Poggioreale, and it should be noted it was not a long street, a crowd of men and pubescent boys had formed behind her, just as the servants and farmhands did on the estate. She had not lost her power by any means; indeed in the confined spaces of the city her scent seemed even more intense than when borne on the breezes in the open country.

Naturally in a large city like Napoli, there was a wide variety of nasal types to be seen. The aquiline, the Roman, the bulbous, the fine, the fat, the crooked, the broken, the hooked, the squashed, the slanted, the big, the small, the moderate. All were represented in the crowd which followed Ramona and each vied with its neighbours for the largest share of the enticing aroma. The sound of sniffing filled the air as the nostrils flared massively. The city had never known anything like it. The owners of the noses closed their eyes in ecstasy at the glimpse of the dream, the magic of the harem, the well of never-ending pleasures that the scent seemed in the brief thread of an instant to offer them.

Ramona was pleased that her powers had not deserted her, yet for the first time the phenomenon scared her. These men were strangers. They were not the familiar band of cowmen and ploughmen she could flatten with a single insult.

As she progressed along the road towards what she thought was the centre of town, Ramona brought the traffic to a halt. The

75

tooting of hooters became deafening as carriage and cart drivers stopped in their tracks. Riders on horseback pulled up. Even the horses lifted their heads and emitted eerie cries, surprised by an aroma which they had never smelled before, but which, somewhere in their evolutionary history, had been known to their ancestors out roaming free in herds on the primeval plains. Dogs too sniffed the air as far as three blocks away, and followed the trail to Ramona. The sound of frenzied barking was painful to the ears.

Ramona walked on, determined to continue with her expedition to the shops; the bonnets and shoes lured her, and the gowns and gloves and parasols were calling out her name. As she increased her pace, so too did her followers, and the dogs in their pack. A truly ridiculous procession entered the Strada di Toledo from the Piazza Dante. All the well-to-do shoppers, the delivery boys, the merchants, the vintners, the shoe-makers, the pharmacists, the waiters and the priests turned to stare at Ramona's retinue, and those who caught up her scent added themselves to their number. In the ensuing mayhem it was difficult for Ramona to make her selections from the glittering windows. She was constantly obliged to move on, for if she remained stationary for long the crowd pressed too tightly around her and prevented her from seeing anything.

She was lured inside Confezione di Spinelli

by glamorous mannequins that were uncannily like real women. The crowd of admirers forced its way in behind her, and there was much jostling and shoving as she made her way to the department displaying the hats. The baker's boys and chimney sweeps and water carriers closed in behind her, watching her carefully. What would this goddess do next?

The grand sales lady did not even deign to look at Ramona, and continued to waft a feather duster amongst the display stands, rearranging a bow here, a bauble there.

'I will try this, this and this,' said Ramona pointing at the most alluring hats she could see.

'Will you indeed?' asked the sales lady impudently. 'And have you got the money to buy these things, my fine lady?' she demanded with a sneer looking at Ramona's pitiful attire, her dowdy gown with its obvious patches, her cheap and ugly bonnet.

'Not today,' answered Ramona truthfully, 'but I will have soon. Just as soon as my husband finds employment.'

'Well, I suggest you come back then,' snapped the sales lady. Immediately she rang a bell and called the floor manager who summoned a bellboy in a smart uniform who ushered Ramona and her retinue of scamps ignominiously out of the store.

CHAPTER TWELVE

THE FONTANA
REFRESHMENT ROOMS

Tears welled inside the eyeglasses as Ramona was shown from the magnificent halls of Spinelli's into the street. The shame of it! Suppose a passing *visconte* should see? It was all a big mistake. She would have the money soon; enough to buy every hat in the shop, and then that cheeky salesgirl would pay for her insolence.

Oh if only Rinaldo had done something sooner, she would have been spared this humiliation. Why had he not arranged to see the employers yesterday as soon as they arrived? He had wasted so much time. He was very much at fault. Just as Ramona was cursing Rinaldo for his sloth, a gentleman approached her and raised his hat to her.

'Signora, I saw what happened in the millinery department of Spinelli's. I must say I thought the salesgirl most impudent. I know Signor Spinelli personally and I shall certainly speak to him about that girl's manners.'

At this, Ramona's eyes grew wide, and she came closer to look at this man who knew Signor Spinelli personally.

'I pray, signora, that you do not distress

yourself over the appalling treatment you received, and allow me to revive you with some coffee.'

He held her arm by the elbow and propelled her across the street to the Fontana Refreshment Rooms. Ramona had never been in refreshment rooms before. She looked around at the gilt fixtures and fittings in awe. There were mirrors everywhere, and she was able to contemplate herself from all angles. Her gown was really very ugly. How remiss of Rinaldo not to get her a better one.

She was shown to a pink velvet banquette in a corner, and the gentleman sat in beside her. It was just like being in a carriage, even grander than the Signora's *carozza*, where she used to bed down with Vittorino Broschi, the pockmarked postilion.

The gentleman was breathing heavily, sucking in Ramona's elixir. He introduced himself as Signor Pastini.

'I am Ramona,' she said grandly and glugged back her coffee in one slug. Unfortunately it burnt her throat and she was obliged to spit it out again over the white starched tablecloth. The ladies taking their coffee nearby gaped with astonishment and tutted to one another loudly.

'Honestly, Modesta, the people they let in here these days,' said an elderly dowager with a monocle to her companion. 'Absolute riffraff. The Fontana is really not what it used to be.'

'Please don't give it a thought,' said the signor, blotting Ramona's bosom with a napkin. 'The waiter will change the cloth.'

A waiter immediately appeared with another snowy cloth and another cup of coffee. This time Ramona drank her coffee more slowly. Watching the way the signor raised his cup to his lips, and after taking a sip replaced it on the saucer that he held in his other hand, she did the same, and felt very pleased with herself.

They chatted about the races and the opera and the Princess Pasqualata's gout, and the last ball at the palace, and the high cost of life in the city. Admittedly the signor did most of the talking, but Ramona joined in enthusiastically with the most outrageous lies, and felt very satisfied indeed with the conversation.

Time passed most agreeably. Then, after Ramona had gobbled up the dainty pastries on the silver tray, the signor made his intentions plain. He asked if she would like to go home with him, for his house was close by, or if she preferred not to go there he could take a room in a hotel.

'Signor, you really are most kind,' she replied. She had heard the Signora use this expression once and had stored it in her memory for future use. 'I am afraid I cannot come home with you to your house or to the hotel today as my husband is expecting me

80

home at any moment.'

'I am sorry to hear that,' said the signor, pulling on his moustaches, 'but please allow me to give you my card. If you ever need any assistance please do call upon me.'

Ramona took the card that was held out to her. It was embossed with gold lettering, which, of course, made no sense to her. The nuns at the covent had tried to teach her to read more than once, but she could never quite grasp those little squiggles in her brain, and the good sisters, their heavenly patience exhausted, eventually stopped trying. Still, Ramona was not going to admit this to the signor. She pocketed the card, bade him goodbye with a curtsy and flounced out of the refreshment rooms, unleashing the uncharitable remarks of the ladies who belonged there. Poor Ramona. Her ears must have stung from the scratches of those she-cats. As for Signor Pastini, he was obliged to vent his ardour on his aged cook, Quintilla, with the result that luncheon was late, putting his wife in an ugly mood for the rest of the afternoon.

Once outside, Ramona studied the card, but could not fathom it and put it away again. Now she sailed along the Strada di Toledo with her head held high. Her encounter with the signor had restored her confidence and she had almost forgotten the ugly incident in the hat department of Spinelli's.

With her thoughts in the clouds, and her steps dogged by a constantly changing retinue, Ramona spent the rest of the day wandering through streets filled with fine clothes and fancy people until the hour when she thought Rinaldo should have returned home from work. She so wanted to boast that she had been into a refreshment room, and to get from him the money for her shopping. After all, she urgently needed to dress appropriately if she was to be taken seriously at the opera house.

By a miracle, Ramona did find her way home again, albeit via a rather circuitous route on which she led her entourage of admirers. She meandered to such an extent that one of the tortoise trainers ran ahead from the rear of the throng to ask if she was lost. Ramona chose to ignore him. She was far too high and mighty now even to discourse with common people. Eventually she came upon the Via Vecchia Poggioreale by pure chance. Rinaldo was right; all in all it had been a very fortuitous day.

Nonna Pino was highly excited by the crowd which followed Ramona to the door. There were not usually crowds jostling along the Via Vecchia Poggioreale. It was not that kind of a street. She clambered onto her chair to address the gathering.

'Perverts. Hairdressers. Popes. I see you. I see your fiendish faces. False prophets. Don't think you can fool me with your masks and teeth. I may be an old woman but I know the way things are.'

'Don't excite yourself, Mother,' shouted Amalasunta, elbowing her way through the crib-makers and octopus-boilers and lemon-men.

'It's rule one hundred and seventy-five,' Amalasunta gestured angrily to Ramona. 'No drawing crowds of men into the street. No carnivals. No uproar. No gatherings. It's forbidden. Strictly disallowed.'

Ramona forced her way inside and left Amalasunta and her mother to supervise the crowd out in the street. The suitors did not seem to know what to do now and most of them drifted away in twos and threes until there was just a handful of boys left in the shadows, hoping against hope to catch a further glimpse of Ramona before nightfall.

On entering the rooms Ramona was surprised to find Rinaldo already there.

'So what work did you find?' was her first question to him. 'Did you become Archbishop or are you a general?'

'Ramona, I'm not going to be made an archbishop or a general. We have to be more realistic.'

'A banker then?'

'You can't become a banker just like that; it's not that easy. Gentlemen are bankers. You have to know people. You have to know business, which I don't. I'm a farmhand,

83

Ramona. I know a bit about keeping bees. I don't know anything about banking.'

Ramona's face was beginning to fall: 'Well are you a cavalry officer, Rinaldo?' she asked, a note of impatience creeping into her voice.

He shook his head.

'An orchestra conductor?'

'No, Ramona, I know nothing of music.'

'A rich merchant then?'

'No.'

'I don't understand what you are telling me, Rinaldo,' she said, shaking her head. 'What work is it that you have taken?'

'Ramona, I wasn't going to tell you this, because I didn't want you to be upset. But as you press me, I have to tell you. I spent all day walking the streets searching for work. I asked everywhere, on building sites, in factories, in hotels, shops, cafés, markets. There wasn't any work. I couldn't find anything.'

'I don't understand you, Rinaldo,' said Ramona, holding her head with her hands as though she was feeling pain. 'You mean you haven't taken any work?'

'I haven't taken any because there was none to be had,' was his reply.

'But Rinaldo, if you haven't found work, how am I going to buy my dresses tomorrow? And if I can't have new dresses how am I to go to the opera house? I can't go in these rags, that's for certain.'

'I'm sorry, Ramona, you won't be able to

buy the dresses tomorrow.'

Ramona's pink eyes were liquid, like small molluscs in their shells. She sniffed hard. 'So when will I be able to buy them Rinaldo?' she asked.

It broke his heart to see her so sad.

'I'll go out again tomorrow, as soon as it gets light. And I'll keep trying until I get something. They say there may be work coming up at a factory in Posillipo. It's a long journey, but I don't mind. Failing that I may be able to get something on the ships; I'll try down at the wharf tomorrow: today there was such a long queue that it was useless to wait.'

'But Rinaldo I don't want you to work in a factory at Posillipo, or on a ship. If you were going to be an admiral it would be different, but an ordinary sailor? It's not right.'

'We need to start somewhere, Ramona. Once we get established, and have a little money, then things will be different and you will be able to go shopping and buy all the beautiful things you want, and you will be able to sing at the opera. But for the moment we just have to take what we can get. You do understand that, don't you, Ramona?'

CHAPTER THIRTEEN

THE HUMPBACK'S PREDICTION

Rinaldo left the house early the following morning with a heavy heart. He had not anticipated that finding work would be so difficult. He walked all the way to Posillipo to avoid unnecessary expense on the tram. But when he got there, there was nothing: the rumours of work at the brush factory were false. And so again he tramped the streets, but without a *raccomandazione* it was a hard task indeed to find work in a city run by favours.

Meanwhile Ramona was putting her own plans into action. Clearly, she could not wait for Rinaldo to find work. Yesterday her faith in him had been shaken. She could not believe his story that there was no work. No work at all, in a city of this size? He was lazy, that was all. And his lack of ambition worried her. She wanted more out of life. She would launch herself into the world and realize her dreams.

As a first step Ramona decided to consult the humpback Rupinello and have him read her fortune. If today was to be a lucky day she would set out immediately for the opera house. Although it was still early she knocked loudly on the door of her neighbour. Surely it was time for him to wake up.

Rupinello was already terribly in love with her. He had been since the first draught of her aroma had penetrated his soft pink nasal passages. Yet he knew in his heart the fundamental truth that Ramona would never return his love. Perhaps she would feel nothing other than pity for him, and then, perhaps, not even that.

He knew that she would use him as best suited her purposes. She would allow him to worship her, allow him to feel, to hope, to dream that his love might be returned, but in truth it could only be scorned. She would exploit him; she would have him run when she beckoned; comfort her when she needed comfort. She would have him bolster her courage at the expense of his own. She would take from him everything he had, and more, without offering anything in return. She would bleed him dry.

Yet, knowing all this he loved her still. More, perhaps, than he would have had it not been so. For men are strange creatures, and love most what is forbidden them.

And so Rupinello, awoken from sleep by an urgent banging, fearing that the house had caught fire or that murderers had got in, opened his door armed with a bottle, to find the subject of his dreams on his threshold. Warm and milky and stretching like a little cat, he stood back to allow Ramona inside.

'Read my fortune, little man,' she

commanded him.

Rupinello rubbed the sleep from his eyes. The aroma was already filling the room with its ripe and unbearable beauty. He breathed deeply. He breathed as though his life depended upon it. The tender passages behind his nose, which in itself was unremarkable— snub and pitted periodically by the scars of an ancient pox—transported the perfume's messages to the sensors in his brain which became steeped with desire like a plum pudding soaked in brandy.

He did not know what to do, and in what order. He wanted to dance, to swim, to sing, to cry, to laugh, to bray like a mule, mew like a cat, hiss like a serpent, erupt like the great volcano itself. But all he could do was slump into a chair before he became obliged to fall, insensible, to the ground. Ramona watched his torment with little sympathy.

'Do get on with it,' she said impatiently, 'I can't wait around all day while you fidget and fuss.'

Rupinello stumbled to the box where he kept the appurtenances of his trade in fortunes: his cards and charms and number blocks. Then he motioned to Ramona to sit opposite him across a little table. He could feel the scent like a force wringing from him his power to live independently as he always had. From now on, for ever, he would be her slave.

He shuffled the cards in his tiny hands,

rhythmically, slowly, seeking to transfer to them his energy, but in truth he had no energy left: the way his body and mind were reacting to Ramona's smell had drained him of all strength. From the pile he took the empress and laid it down on the table in front of Ramona.

'Is that me?' she asked.

Rupinello nodded gravely. Then, having shuffled the remaining cards once more, he laid them out on the table according to the ancient lore.

The first card was the judgment: the judgment that lay in store for Ramona. The next card would reveal what this judgment was to be.

He turned it: the nine of swords, for agony and misery. Rupinello shuddered.

'Is it bad?'

'No,' he lied, 'not bad. It's just the cards don't talk to me today. Let me see your palm instead.'

Ramona held out her palm. If anything it read worse than the cards. Torment, misery, madness, despair, death. All were here, plain as day. Rupinello rubbed his eyes; they were blurry from sleep, that was it.

'Is it not good?' asked Ramona eventually.

'Oh yes, it is. It is good,' Rupinello lied. How could he tell her the truth?

'And so what does it say? Will it be a good day today? Will I be successful at the opera house? Will I be made the prima donna?'

'Most certainly.'

'Then I must go,' said Ramona standing up, 'I can't waste any more time. I must go at once to the San Carlo. You are a very good fortune teller. You tell it just as it is, not like the others. They just tell the bad things, not the good. You really tell the truth, I know.'

She gave him a little kiss for his efforts, little enough to be almost nothing, but it was something to him, and then she swept out of the room, her courage bolstered.

When she had gone, Rupinello crumpled. Why was he so short and deformed with a hump? Surely if he looked different she would love him.

He had abused his gift and told lies, and he felt bad. But he couldn't tell her the truth. Idly his fingers strayed to the card left unturned on the top of the pack when he had stopped dealing. The fool. Was he the fool?

Exhausted, Rupinello crept back between the covers of his little bed. Today had not started well. He would wait for tomorrow before emerging once more into that brutal world.

CHAPTER FOURTEEN

THE AUDITION

Now Ramona was determined to seize the moment. She left the apartment bursting with the urgency of the inspired. Nonna Pino spotted her, and brandishing a huge and unwieldy crucifix she cried: 'She-Devil. Body snatcher. Here comes the bride of Lucifer!'

This time Ramona ignored the madwoman, focusing instead on the next step in her strategy. Since she could not audition for a part at the opera dressed in tatters, she would borrow a fancy dress from Tebaldi's rag shop, which she had passed by on her circular walk along the Via Acquaviva.

Policarpo Tebaldi was just opening his shutters as Ramona strode up, trailing a few stray potmen and undertakers in her wake. Policarpo Tebaldi was not slow to inhale the scent. Shooing her followers away like flies, he led Ramona into the shop and shut the door. Ramona told him what she needed, though she did not reveal her true purpose, and Policarpo Tebaldi produced a selection of his stock. It was not much, but Ramona had learned a little how to compromise and felt that anything was better than what she already had.

By a stroke of good fortune Brunella Tosti,

the whore who lived above the shop, had fallen on hard times and had been obliged to sell off some of her items to pay her escalating debts. Hence there was a royal blue gown in a cheap and scratchy satin with a matching feather boa, and a dented top hat in a violently contrasting shade of green. Ramona was delighted: she had never worn things so beautiful. She seized the garments and made her way to the fitting room at the rear of the shop which Policarpo Tebaldi had so rigged up with a series of angled mirrors that he was able to see everything as she took her clothes off.

Ramona struggled into the gown. She and Brunella Tosti were of different shapes and sizes, that much was evident. Brunella must have been a good head taller and half the width, but Ramona squeezed and tugged and ripped seams until she was inside, and to her eyes the results were magical. She was transformed by the finery. Never had she seen herself like this. Looking like a whore, Ramona felt like a queen. She donned the hat to complete the ensemble and emerged from the fitting room for Policarpo Tebaldi's approval, which he was not slow in providing. To be frank, he was foaming at the mouth. The whole of the grubby little shop was bathed in the gold of Ramona's scent: the sad rags looked new; the filth had acquired its own charm, like little piles of fairy dust. Even the rats looked more friendly.

And so, leaving her own clothes and two *carlini* which she had taken from Rinaldo's secret security fund, Ramona set off to try her luck at the opera house. Policarpo Tebaldi lost no time in assuming Ramona's cast-off clothes himself: thus he could feel her scent all around him and almost imagine he was inside her skin.

Emerging into the daylight, Ramona adjusted the eyeglasses and wondered which route to take.

'Five grains,' offered a passing postman.

'Six,' topped an offal vendor, balancing his tray of entrails on his head.

Ramona looked at them blankly. What were they talking about? Honestly, there were such strange people in the city.

She set off in the direction in which she supposed the grand San Carlo opera house lay. Unfortunately she had chosen the very opposite way and was in fact heading towards the prison. Quickly a crowd gathered around her: saucepan menders, scissor sharpeners, cut-throats. Ramona tossed her head and stepped out as fast as she possibly could; if she was quick she could make her début in tonight's performance. She would need to have costume fittings, but they were sure to have something in their extensive wardrobes that would do her justice; not that she would agree to wear just anything. No, indeed: she intended to act like a real star and be difficult when it was required.

The crowd, thickened by the addition of glow-worm vendors, transvestites, and professional mourners from the city's three hundred funeral parlours, hurried along behind her, braying:

'How much do you charge?'

'I'll pay anything.'

'Seven grains.'

'Eight.'

'Nine.'

'Will you take a fresh sea bass in exchange?'

'I'll give you a sheep's head.'

'As much lemonade as you can drink.'

Ramona ignored them. These vulgar people made her feel sick. When she reached the towering iron walls of the prison, she realized she had taken the wrong road and did an abrupt about-turn, which left the crowd in confusion. The admirers pushed and pulled in all directions but stayed together as though joined by elastic. For a moment sight of Ramona was lost. Suddenly an egg merchant who was unusually tall spotted her train of dazzling blue disappearing around the corner of the Via Giovanni Porzio, and a race started amongst the fleet of foot to see who would reach her first.

Ramona picked up speed, so intent was she upon her purpose. She crossed the Piazza Garibaldi at a run and raced along the Corso Umberto. She was surprised at how far it was, but determination gave wings to her feet.

Eventually the throng arrived at the San Carlo, and Ramona shook out her skirts and adjusted the hat before climbing the steps to the entrance.

The concierge approached and with one slow suck of breath through his magnificent nose knew immediately that his whole life had been, until this moment, a tragic sham. He breathed in Ramona's scent and understood the universe. That evening he went home and bludgeoned his wife to death with a candlestick. It was the only way he could bear it.

He raised his hand in a silent gesture, and thus held back the throng of bootblacks who surged in behind Ramona. They understood the sign and stopped. Seeing a commotion on the steps of the opera house, some officers of the *carabinieri* approached and taking in hand their batons sought to disperse the gathering of footpads and rapscallions and restore order. Fifty-seven arrests were made as grown men clung to the railings, sobbing to be allowed to stay where they were for the rest of their lives.

Inside, Ramona explained to the concierge that she wished to audition. He bowed and ushered her through corridors lined with carpet so thick it felt like the grass in the Signora's garden. If only the Signora could see her now. Would she be jealous? The walls were lined with portraits of the famous singers: Melba, Patti, Anselmi, the great Caruso himself. Soon Ramona's likeness would be amongst them.

After walking for some time they reached the offices of Signor Giambattista Po, the artistic director. What a sight met his eyes! At first he thought it was a joke, but then he inhaled. He stood up and the scent knocked him backwards with all of its force and dropped him once more into his chair. He was ready to lie down on the carpet and roll over onto his back like a puppy, playfully wagging his tail. Yet this did not prove necessary, for Ramona was willing to do what was required, anything, in fact, to further her plans.

'How can I be of assistance, signorina?' he asked, coming forward and reaching for her hand. Seated behind his majestic desk he seemed a man of great stature, but when he emerged from its confines it became apparent that he was no taller than a boy.

'I am Ramona Drottoveo,' she said in an affected voice. 'I have come to sing.'

'I see,' replied Signor Po as the gift dropped into his lap. 'And may I ask, Signorina Drottoveo, where you trained? Was it perhaps La Scala, or . . .?' he let the question trail off as he undressed Ramona with his eyes, stripping away the cheap frippery and picturing the plump pink cheeks of her buttocks, her sturdy legs.

'Trained?' asked Ramona in confusion.

'Surely your voice was trained in one of the

96

great academies, signorina? Or perhaps you trained abroad?'

Ramona grew hot and uncomfortable. She had not expected to be asked a lot of questions. She looked down at the carpet and thought about crying.

'So perhaps, your voice is as yet untrained, signorina?'

Ramona looked up and nodded.

'Well, so much the better. A voice in its natural state. A wild flower is so much sweeter than one forced up in the hothouse, if you will allow me to say so. If you have talent, and looking at you Signorina Drottoveo, it is abundantly clear to me that you do, the little matter of a lack of training, why, it is nothing. Nothing at all.'

'I want to sing,' she said, feeling she had cleared the first hurdle.

'Of course you do,' he said, nodding in agreement; it was the most natural thing in the world. 'And you have come to the right place, because I am just the man to help you.'

'You are?' she asked with joy in her voice.

'Yes, I am,' said the signor as he locked his office door from the inside and pocketed the key.

'Why do you lock the door, signor?' she asked.

'Why because I am going to ask you to perform for me a little, signorina, to show me a little of what you can do, so I can help you.

97

We don't want to be disturbed, do we?' he asked. 'Not while you are showing me your wonderful talents.'

As he was saying this, Signor Po approached Ramona and without hesitation or introduction he buried his head in her bosom, all the better to ingest the smell of her skin. Oh what sweet suffocation! He was drowning in her very essence; swimming in it; swallowing it. He uttered groans and moans of deepest pleasure. He did not even notice at the time how the cheap satin grazed his skin. The following day, however, he was to come out in an unsightly rash which would linger for several weeks. Then without emerging from the succulent pool, he executed a little fancy footwork—not for nothing had he begun his career as a dancer—and manoeuvred Ramona across the room so that all at once and without being aware of the motion, she found herself prostrate on his sofa.

'And will I be in this evening's performance, signor?' she asked as he climbed astride her, with his head still buried in her cleavage.

'There is no need to rush, signorina,' came the muffled reply. 'Let us just take our time. I have to know exactly where your talents lie so I can know the right part to give you. Relax, signorina, we will discuss the details later.'

And so Ramona allowed the artistic director to make a thorough assessment of her talents. He immersed himself totally in the fountainhead of the maddening aroma, and finally, crying with rapture, he blended with it the meagre spurt of his own little wellspring.

While he did so Ramona lay back unmoved and consoled herself with thoughts of how soon she, Ramona Drottoveo, would be the star of the performance. She would be the talk of Napoli. Surely then she would receive invitations to the wonderful parties and circuses and dances that she knew were happening all over the city.

When he had transcended the soaring heights of pleasure which Ramona had aroused within him, the signor fell into a dead faint from which there was no waking him. Ramona shook him and slapped him to no avail. Finally, having tried all the usual methods, she was left with no alternative but to douse him liberally with the cold water from a vase of flowers.

The signor spluttered back to life, and was clearly piqued by Ramona's chosen method of resuscitation and the resultant ruined suit, because his face turned purple, and his nose throbbed. Alarmed by the passage of time, he then made haste to remove Ramona from his office. He knew that his absence would by now have been noted by his enemies. Those vipers Fanzago and Bottiglieri were simply waiting for one last transgression before using their knowledge to have him ousted by the Board. He would not go without a fight, they could be sure of that.

'Thank you so much, Signorina Drottoveo,' he said briskly, removing a chrysanthemum from his waistcoat and unlocking the office door. Outside, the caretaker, Panfilo, made an elaborate show of polishing the doorknob as the odd couple emerged, Po dripping a trail of greenish water, fern and dwarf agapanthus.

'You there, clean this mess up,' the artistic director barked at Panfilo, swiping at his suit to remove the last traces of the petals.

'But signor, you haven't even asked me to sing,' said Ramona as she found herself propelled towards the exit.

'There is no need, signorina, I know all I need to know. I have to confess that all the positions of opera singer are full at this time. Regrettably this is the case, and I cannot create a vacancy where none exists. No, not even for such a charming and talented girl as you are. But as soon as there is an opening I will call for you in my carriage and you will be the star of the performance. Thank you very much for coming in. Good day.'

With that he kissed Ramona's hand and vanished before she could say another word. Certainly the audition had been irregular: she knew there should have been some need for her to sing. She was somewhat disappointed, but she believed everything Signor Po told her. If there were no vacancies, she could not appear; but very soon she would be up there on the stage as the leading soprano. On the whole, all things considered, she was pleased with her afternoon's work, and was confidently expecting to be summoned to the theatre for her début on the following day. A vacancy was sure to have arisen by then.

CHAPTER FIFTEEN

THE OPERA

The following day Ramona did receive her summons to the San Carlo. She had been standing at the window practising *Una voce poco fa* and other songs she had heard at musical evenings given by the Signora for her provincial friends. They were not terribly faithful renditions of the original pieces, but Ramona endowed them with her own charm. The passers-by looked up at the sound of the cracked notes and shook their heads in a pained way. Some even laughed.

As she brandished her fist at a particularly vociferous fisherwife who was complaining that the noise had poisoned her squid, Ramona noticed a smart carriage draw into the Via Vecchia Poggioreale from the direction of the Via Arenaccia. It was drawn by four black horses with plumes of blue feathers on their heads. The driver was in a livery also of blue, edged with gold, and Ramona noticed that there were two footmen at the rear, wearing the same livery and tall helmets. The carriage itself was gleaming. It was of a dark wood with a golden crest, and the harness and everything was just to Ramona's liking. Indeed it was just the kind of carriage she herself would have chosen in which to parade around the city during the *passeggiata*.

She watched the carriage draw along the street. Not many fine carriages were seen in this part of town; indeed this was the first that Ramona had seen since she had been in residence here.

Instead of driving past, the carriage stopped in front of the house. The footmen dismounted, opened the door on the near side and let down the folding steps. Then, who should emerge from the carriage but Signor Po himself! Ramona was not surprised. She had been expecting him. Instinctively she adjusted her hair, and continued to watch as the street urchins and the vicious women who were her neighbours crowded around the carriage, smearing the gleaming woodwork with their greasy fingers and begging for alms.

Signor Po waved them away with a gloved hand. Those whom Ramona especially disliked, and the Castorellis were included in this number, he had whipped by his coachman. Nonna Pino was beaten relentlessly until she lay in a mangled heap in the dirt. Ramona cheered at this; looking up, and seeing her at her top floor window, the signor raised his hat and made an elaborate bow.

The Castorellis, beaten but still obsequious, grovellingly showed him inside their humble dwelling and led him up the stinking stairway to where she, Ramona, was ready to receive him.

'I have come for you, Signorina Drottoveo,' he said simply, and drew her down from her apartment into his waiting carriage. The harlots and brothel keepers and moneylenders stared as Ramona was whisked away to a new life of ease and luxury that they could only dream about.

Signor Po tried to make love to Ramona in the carriage. She was teasing but firm in her response. She told him she was a married woman and that although she was anxious to do all she could to advance her career, it was by her singing that she wished to win fame from now on. Tears formed in the signor's eyes at this but he admired her resolution, and silently he prayed to the Holy Virgin to send him a similarly virtuous bride.

The carriage sped through the streets like an arrow and soon arrived in the Via San Carlo. Already a crowd had gathered to applaud the new diva, and Ramona waved at the princes and barons and dukes who had assembled on the steps of the *teatro* to catch a glimpse of her before she was swept along by an army of liveried ushers into the foyer. How many crowns and coronets almost came to blows in their urgency to gain her notice!

The speed with which she was delivered up into the star's dressing room for costume fittings made her giddy, and in seconds she was arrayed in finery by a troupe of seventeen dressers. Once Ramona was bedecked, the dressers stood back to admire her, and they all began to weep, such a vision did Ramona appear in her finery.

Ramona surveyed herself in a full-length looking glass at the far end of the dressing room. It confirmed what she had always known: she was magnificent. It had only taken the right clothes to reveal the dizzying heights of her beauty, just as a jewel needs to be polished and mounted in a precious setting before it can truly dazzle.

Signor Po was allowed in. He then passed out, susceptible to fainting fits as he was. Ramona was just looking round for a vase of flowers when a squadron of servants rushed in and brought him around by the liberal application of smelling salts and brandy. The signor's second-best suit was saved.

'Signorina Drottoveo,' he gasped when he had regained consciousness, 'I have never seen a vision of loveliness to compare with you.'

Ramona blew him a coquette's kiss of thanks before the dressers surrounded her and had her decked out in the next costume for the second act, and so on, and each one was more lovely than the last. Ramona preened and paraded like a peacock.

Then, suddenly, it was time for rehearsals and she was swept by the tide of officials up the stairs to backstage. The lights came on, the orchestra struck up the overture, the curtains opened, and there she was, Ramona Drottoveo on centre stage at the San Carlo. It was a defining moment. All strained forward to hear the first sound. Ramona opened her lips, and right on cue came the most pure and beautiful note that had ever been formed by a human voice. Ramona sang her way through aria after aria, and as she grew in confidence her voice soared like a dove to the heavens, and even the deaf caretaker, Panfilo, mopping the floors at the very back, abandoned his mop and bucket and wept.

Even though it was only a dress rehearsal, when the final note of Ramona's crystal throat had died hauntingly away, the bouquets thrown by the staff cascaded onto the stage and Ramona curtsied low with her eyes closed. Tears had formed tiny pools in the tight rubber surrounds of the eyeglasses. Shivers tingled down her spine. Finally Ramona Drottoveo had arrived.

Signor Po, as he made his way towards her across a stage strewn with freesia and roses and violets, was by now a gibbering wreck.

Words could not express his emotion and he blubbed incomprehensibly into a silk handkerchief. It was the dream of all artistic directors of the opera come true, and he, he, Giambattista Po, had made the discovery. Ramona Drottoveo was his, all his.

Before she knew it, it was time for the evening performance. Word had circulated throughout the city and not a single one of the theatre's three thousand seats was empty.

Ramona was almost ready. A team of hairdressers had been at work on her silvery hair and had formed it into an exquisite mound like *gelato*, topped with the tiara. Her face was painted and powdered to a white finish which made her look most unlike her normal pink self. They had tried to remove her eyeglasses, but the bright lights hurt her eyes and so she was allowed to wear them after all, for they could not risk displeasing the prima donna.

Ramona felt coloured butterflies of excitement fluttering their wings in her stomach as she made her way through the labyrinth of scenery backstage. Her moment had come. She was led out to her opening position and then they left her unattended on the stage that was as big as a piazza. She had never felt so entirely alone. She smoothed the folds of her gown, stood up straight, stomach in, deep breath, ready. The lights came on and shone brightly in her eyes. Surely she had not left her eyeglasses behind?

'Ramona,' came a voice she recognized. But what was it doing here, backstage at the opera house? It was Rinaldo's voice.

'Ramona, help me, I had the most horrible nightmare. The beekeeper was here, actually in the room. He was watching us.' In the light of the lamp he had lit, Rinaldo looked ashen. His eyes were circles of pure fear, and he was gasping for breath.

Ramona was struggling to understand what was happening. How had she been so suddenly transported from the glittering San Carlo to the cold, depressing tenement in the Via Vecchia Poggioreale? Where were the pretty dresses? Here she looked down at herself and saw she had, like Cinderella, resumed her rags. Where was the bouffant hairdo? She felt for the tiara: it was gone from her head. Where was the orchestra? The crowds? The adulation? The flowers? The champagne? The butterflies?

All of it gone. And she back in her horrid life in the blinking of an eye. How she cried when she realized that it had all been a dream. She scratched Rinaldo, and bit him too. It was all his fault. If he had not woken her when he did she would be singing right now. Her true moment of glory had been denied her. It had all been a dream. A beautiful, beautiful dream.

CHAPTER SIXTEEN

RINALDO BECOMES POSSESSED

Had Ramona been more sensible she might have begun to realize that she had been deceived: that Signor Po was simply toying with her, amusing himself for an afternoon between appointments. She was never going to receive the summons to the San Carlo.

Yet it was characteristic of Ramona's boneheadedness that she would argue against herself in such circumstances and insist on winning. Accordingly, if anything, her confidence in Signor Po increased, and she would not hear herself think a thought against him. In fact, in her benevolent memory, his willy grew in size to one that any man would have been proud of.

Rinaldo had still not managed to find a job. He didn't give up looking, and spent every day out trudging the streets, but his hope was fading. All their money was gone, and Ramona had started borrowing from Rupinello to pay their expenses, which made Rinaldo feel terrible. He had never borrowed in his life. Ramona was always rebuking him for his failure to buy her the fripperies she said she had been promised, and he had begun to feel depressed.

His sleep was often disturbed by nightmares. At night he would call upon the Seven Sleepers of Ephesus to bring him rest, but invariably, as soon as he closed his eyes, he was visited by the undead beekeeper, and the buzzing bees with Ramona's face. A burden of guilt was growing inside him like a cancer. In time Rinaldo came to feel that he had become possessed by the spirit of the dead man.

One evening he went into the church near the apartment, the Chiesa di Santa Maria del Fede. He did not know quite why he went inside. He was not a religious man: he had not been inside a church in years except for his wedding to Ramona. But soon Rinaldo found himself kneeling at the confessional pouring out his heart to the priest, Padre Buonconte.

'Yours was a grave sin, my son,' said the padre when Rinaldo had concluded his tale. 'A grave sin. It's no wonder the spirit of the wronged beekeeper will not rest, and follows you, wanting redress. You stole his bride. Why, he finds you in his bed with her the day after the wedding? Soon after that he is discovered dead, driven by despair to take his own life. A terrible sin. He does not receive the last rites, he dies without repentance. Then the body disappears and is denied burial. Oh, what a soul in torment! It is no surprise to me that he haunts you, for in his eyes it was you who sent him to his death.'

'I know it, Father,' Rinaldo sobbed behind

109

his hands. 'I bear the guilt and hate myself for what I have done.'

'But what about the young woman?' asked the priest. 'Does she not repent?'

'My wife is not to blame. She is a child, Father, an innocent, she has committed no sin. It is I, I alone who am guilty. And I must pay the price.'

'But she is guilty of adultery, my son. She played her part in this terrible affair. You cannot assume the weight of her sin. Only the Lord our God can absolve us. You must bring her to confession, for if she does not repent she cannot be saved.'

'I will try to bring her,' said Rinaldo without conviction, knowing Ramona's views on the clergy all too well. 'But what about the spirit, Padre?' he added, his fear of the approaching night making him shiver.

'I will call tomorrow evening at your home and conduct the rites of exorcism. Perhaps then we may lay this tortured soul to rest. Now go in peace and expect me tomorrow, when I will have prepared my soul and my body by fasting.'

Rinaldo left the church, feeling that even if the priest could free him from the spirit of the beekeeper, they should take this as a warning and leave Napoli. Maybe they should head back to the estate. Perhaps the steward would relent on hearing of their ill luck in the city, and would agree to take them back. It was worth a try.

Ramona, however, would not hear a word about returning to the estate; indeed she blocked her ears with her fingers when Rinaldo even touched on the subject. Her pride would never allow her to admit that their journey to the city had been unsuccessful. Besides, she did not accept that it had. Any day now she would be appearing at the opera house, and then Rinaldo would be forced to eat his words. She would not have the women on the estate poke their fingers at her and laugh in her face; she would die first. And she loved it in the city; she simply loved it. How could Rinaldo, who pretended to love her, wish to take her away from the place where she was happiest in the whole world? To remove her would be to kill her, she was convinced of that.

'Ramona, I love you more than life itself,' said Rinaldo, lacerated by the implication that he did not love her.

'Then make me happy,' she said simply.

Rinaldo could do nothing but comply with her wishes, and against his better judgment he agreed that they could stay. Later, he told her of his arrangement with Padre Buonconte.

'I won't have any priests in here,' said Ramona flatly.

'But he's a good man. He will help us.'

'We must help ourselves, Rinaldo. Priests will do us no good.'

111

'But Ramona, how are we going to rid ourselves of the spirit that haunts us?'

'What spirit? I see no spirits. It's you, Rinaldo. I think you're going mad. Guendalina Fumagalli, the laundry maid, went mad. It was just before you came to La Casa. She chewed up all the fresh linen in the store cupboard. You should have seen the Signora! They took her away to the *manicomio* at Carinola. They cut all her hair off and eventually she swallowed her own tongue and died. And I can't be sure of this, but I think, if you do go mad, really mad, Rinaldo, I don't think I will love you any more.'

'Oh Ramona, how can you say you'll stop loving me? I'm not going mad. I just want to change things, make them better, make us happy again. There's something wrong here. Something bad.'

'There is nothing bad. It's all nonsense. Now let's drop it, shall we? I'm getting a headache, and I won't be able to sing tomorrow if I have a headache.'

'I think it's you who's going mad,' said Rinaldo in a rare moment of temper. She glared at him, daring him to continue what he had started. He had gone too far now to hold back. He let it out.

'They're never going to let you sing at the opera.'

Ramona turned her back on him and did not speak to him for days. She now bore a little

112

piece of grit in her heart towards Rinaldo which would never go away.

CHAPTER SEVENTEEN

THE EXORCISM

The following evening the priest came wearing the appointed violet-coloured stole, and despite Ramona's reluctance he performed the rites of exorcism.

As soon as he entered the apartment, Ramona's scent penetrated the nostrils of the priest and he feared the temptation of the devil. In silent prayer he beseeched the Holy Virgin to save him, but even she could not prevent his body from responding to the irreverent aroma in the only way it could. Beginning that very night, he vowed to atone for his weakness by scourging himself with willow branches and dousing himself with iced water for a period of forty days.

Ramona stood sullenly by as Padre Buonconte unpacked his little bag of tricks. All the while his loins throbbed, and a sweat stood upon his brow. The devil was all around him, he could feel, taunting him, tempting him. With trembling fingers he withdrew his bells, candles, the crucifix and a vessel of holy water. He had even brought along some relics of the saints. With a flourish he produced the finger of Santa Maria Margherita, who oversees the rite of exorcism. The finger was black and withered and made Ramona recoil. Finally he unpacked censers and a bible. The smell filled his head, and he wrestled in vain with impure thoughts.

'Lord deliver me from temptation,' he whispered over and over, under his breath. Lighting the incense, he swung the censer into every corner, seeking to blot out Ramona's fleshy scent.

Yet the incense could make no progress in the face of such competition. Ramona's aroma responded to the challenge and magnified itself a hundredfold. It penetrated the entire Villaria district, and brought a crowd of men to the street, bigger than any that had followed Ramona in previous days. They stood outside the building in an awed silence.

Inside, Padre Buonconte was sprinkling the holy water liberally around. He was unable to concentrate and the floor was soon drenched. Repeatedly he tried to remind himself of his purpose. Under his breath he murmured the words of the litany and called on the restless spirit of the beekeeper to depart, but he could not do it with any degree of conviction. He knew that if he were a restless spirit, wandering the earth, he too would choose to reside in this apartment where the aroma offered its own heaven on earth.

Waging an internal war with himself, the padre made a heroic effort, and seized the large wooden crucifix. He held it at arm's length above his head, mustering his courage.

'Beekeeper,' he spoke out in a resounding voice. 'Beekeeper, we pray to the saints for intercession. We pray that your restless spirit may pass through Purgatory and eventually find peace with Our Lord. This is not the place appointed for you. I call upon you to be gone in the name of the Holy Mother. Be gone to where your soul will be purified of its sins thence to pass into the kingdom of grace for ever. Be gone in the name of Our Lady.'

Rinaldo fervently crossed himself. Ramona folded her arms over her chest and resolutely said nothing.

The effort had taken its toll upon the priest, who, it must be said, was no longer a young man, and he staggered under the weight of the mighty crucifix. The scent had made him drunk. His strength was gone. He collapsed onto his knees on the wet floor and sobbed. Rinaldo too fell to his knees, thinking it was part of the ceremony. Ramona saw the bulge under the priest's cassock, and sneered. They were all the same, these men of God.

Outside, the crowd grew restless. The Castorellis were profiting from the situation and the cold night by selling jugs of hot soup and diluted wine which they dispensed from a trestle table in front of the house. Nonna Pino too took advantage of the quasi-religious fervour amongst the crowd to collect for the upkeep of her shrine. In fact she made much more money than San Gennaro in his gaudy niche could ever need. She put away a tidy sum for herself in the stocking she kept hidden in her night commode, away from her prowling son-in-law.

In time, the priest emerged from his meditations. The man of God opened his eyes and saw before him the figure of Ramona. With a start he made haste to cross himself, thinking her, in his confused state, the devil incarnate. Then the padre turned his attention to Rinaldo, who was possessed by the restless spirit. He sprinkled Rinaldo with what little of the holy water remained and, taking up the saint's finger, which resembled a blackened boar's-meat sausage, he applied it to all the areas of Rinaldo's person, uttering these words:

'May the Holy Virgin abide with you in your going out and your coming in. By day and by night, at morning and evening, at all times and in all places may she protect and defend you from the wrath of evil man. From the assaults of evil spirits, from foes, visible and invisible, from the snares of the devil, from all low passions that beguile the soul and body, may she guard, protect and deliver you. Amen.'

'Amen,' Rinaldo responded.

Finally, his faith shaken, the priest gathered

up his implements and left the building. Outside he was jostled by the crowd that had suddenly come to life. The spell was broken.

'What went on within, Padre?' chorused the voices of a thousand boilermen, haberdashers and acrobats.

The priest, without uttering a word, stumbled through their ranks as if in a dream.

The scent was waning, and the nasal passages of the inhabitants of the district began to shrink to their former dimensions.

Inside, in the adjoining apartment, Rupinello collapsed on his bed, drowned in the aroma. He could no longer think. He had become a dumb and desperate beast, lowing blindly in the meadow of his own impotence. He wanted to rip the flesh from his chest with his claws, pluck his eyes from his head, but he did not know why. He slumped down behind the door of his room with his nose to the crack above the threshold, like a dog that detects the passing scent of a bitch. There he lay sniffing hard until the perfume subsided and the ecstasy was over. Eventually sleep crept upon his toy body where it lay hunched in the crack, and when morning woke him from a thick and dreamless night, every part of him hurt with the remembered agony of torture.

The Castorellis dismantled the trestle table and carried the soup tureen and the empty bottles and cups back inside. Although it was their usual practice to curse their tenants, they had to thank Ramona for this unexpected windfall. The prospect of future money-making schemes kept them awake for hours.

Nonna Pino was also restless. Once she was secure in the knowledge that her son-in-law was safely in his bed, she slipped noiselessly out of her own and recovered her bag of gold from the commode. Lovingly she fingered her coinage in the dark, blissfully unaware that her son-in-law knew all about her hiding place and was simply biding his time before swooping down upon it.

Padre Buonconte passed through the thinning crowd in the Via Vecchia Poggioreale a changed man. He staggered back to the *chiesa* and prostrated himself on the floor before the altar in silent discourse with the Lord. His aged frame throbbed with pain. The following morning the sexton found him there, stiff and cold: though long dead, his eyes still poured forth tears.

This phenomenon came to be known as Padre Buonconte's miracle, and it was not long before a cult developed and hordes of the faithful were flocking to the *chiesa* to see the tears for themselves. Even after the interment of the corpse in the crypt, the tears continued to well up and form a pool on the floor of the church. The tears were held to have healing properties, and pilgrims travelled from as far afield as Salerno and Avellino to immerse their gangrenous legs and ulcerated armpits in the *pozza dolorosa*. Amalasunta Castorelli, as befits a woman of commerce, was not slow to set up a stall outside the church where she offered for sale vials of bogus tears, and in the cult's heyday she was selling out of her stocks faster than her husband could draw up the brackish water from the well.

CHAPTER EIGHTEEN

A BABY

Shortly after the exorcism, Ramona made the discovery that she was with child. This came as a shock to her as she had long practised those arts that prevent conception. However there was no mistaking it, and indeed she was fairly far advanced into her pregnancy.

She wasn't pleased at the prospect of having a child, of becoming fat and going through the pain of labour. In addition she felt that this would be the final nail in the coffin of her opera dreams. If Signor Po did send for her, and found her swollen, surely he would not take her and make her a star.

Then she thought about Rinaldo. Despite the terrible price paid by the priest, the exorcism had not succeeded in ridding him of the spectre of the beekeeper. If anything, it had the opposite effect and he had become more and more preoccupied with thoughts of the dead man.

But maybe Rinaldo would be pleased at the news and resolve to resist the progress of the malady which day by day was softening his brain. Could the birth of their child bring them the happiness that was at present eluding them? Could she somehow rekindle the love she had once felt for Rinaldo? Could they become a happy family?

She ran to find Rupinello to have him read the answers to these questions in his crystal ball. Rupinello, struggling not to betray his horror at what the clouded glass was telling him, once again reassured Ramona that all would be as she hoped.

When Rinaldo came home that night she broke the news open for him like a softly boiled egg. It took some moments for him to react, for as usual he was swatting imaginary bees.

'It's the beekeeper's child,' he replied with wild eyes.

Ramona said nothing more. She knew then that it was over, for her and Rinaldo. What had happened to the man she had once known, and loved, and longed for? Where had their love gone? How could it have ended? It was but a paper shadow against a wall, vanishing with the sun, leaving nothing but memories and the pulse of life that was swelling swiftly within her belly.

120

'The crystal ball didn't tell it true, Rupinello,' she reproached him later. 'Rinaldo cares nothing for the baby. He thinks only of the beekeeper.'

'I will always take care of you, Ramona,' murmured the humpback, his eyes filled with the liquid light of love which was causing his lips to froth. 'You and the baby.'

Ramona rewarded him with a little kiss to the forehead. As she leaned over him, a cloud of her fragrance was released from the warm place between her breasts and it clung to Rupinello's body like syrup.

Ramona grew fatter and fatter at an alarming pace. As she did so she indulged herself in every kind of delicacy she craved without thinking of the expense. Sometimes she would wake up in the dead of night with a violent craving for little dumplings in sauce or a steaming rabbit stew. She had only to rap on the partition and call through her order and Rupinello would raise himself from the fetid warmth of his little cot and trot out in the cold and dark to provide her with whatever her heart, or, as some said, her greed, desired.

Rinaldo, although still sharing the bed with Ramona, slept through the crisis. He would rouse from the depths of his stupor only to converse with the beekeeper who still haunted his thoughts, buried though they were beneath the scattered remnants of his mind.

Meanwhile, outside, Rupinello foraged for

food. At that hour, of course, there were no cook shops open, and there were one or two occasions when, after unsuccessful attempts to find the desired dish, he was forced to return to his mistress with empty hands.

He would never, even if he lived to be a hundred, which he knew he never would from reading his own fortune, forget those awful nights. The curses Ramona placed upon him with venom dripping from her tongue, the bites and scratches she inflicted in her fury upon his defenceless body: he still bore the scars. Worse than this, far worse, was his misery at failing to give his beloved what she wanted. How he hated himself for his failure and for making her unhappy.

And so, in time, Rupinello was obliged to enter into an expensive arrangement with a local *rosticceria*. A cook was placed on standby throughout the night should there arise a sudden need for some ribs of pork in Marco Polo sauce or succulent meatballs in gravy, and to the satisfaction of all, there was no recurrence of the ugly scenes. Back in the apartment Ramona could not rest until Rupinello returned with a steaming *pentola* in his arms. She would fall upon him, wrestle the pot from his grasp, and without a word of thanks immediately cram the food into her mouth as though she were suffering from the most severe case of starvation.

Rupinello would watch her with delight, in

the way that people find joy

elephant being fed at the zoo,

humble pig slurping its swill in the

back of the house. Perhaps it grati

humpback to feel that by eating the fo

had got for her she was somehow tak

something of him into herself. That perhaps h

was entering her through the medium of the

pork chops or the pan-fried chicken in the way

that he most wanted to, and in the way which

he knew he would never be permitted.

To indulge Ramona's appetite, Rupinello
plied his hump in the busy byways of the city
from dawn to dusk. He cut prices to attract
customers from his fellow humpbacks, thus
alienating himself from the guild he had been
so proud to enter as a boy. Without the
support of the fraternity he soon became prey
to the Camorra and was obliged to give over a
proportion of his income in protection fees.
Some days his hump was rubbed so sore it
bled, but it still wasn't enough. Once his
meagre savings were gone, he sold off the few
items he had that were worth anything. His
confirmation suit went to Policarpo Tebaldi's
rag shop. He gave up a miniature portrait of
his mother, who had died at the time of his
twisted birth, with much sorrow in exchange
for a few coins.

But the proceeds from the sale of these
items were so quickly spent that Rupinello
knew he had to come up with something else,

ening job at the Circo
ermanently stationed in
onte. He was fired from
s in each performance,
aturdays when there was
e there was a shortage of
and as Rupinello was
Everardo Donadio, the
give him a try. It was a
wise decision, for the paying public loves a
humpback, and a flying one was a greater
attraction still.

Soon the noise of the gunpowder exploding
at close range began to dull Rupinello's
hearing. But as he soared through the choking
smoke in the tent before landing in the safety
net held out for him by the troupe of clowns
his only thought was of Ramona. In the
shaving of the second before he plummeted to
the ground he imagined himself swimming in
the crystal pool of her aroma, forming long
striding strokes with his arms, flipping onto his
back and kicking his legs, making a lot of
splash. Then he would land in the net and
suddenly the world was divided by squares of
string. He struggled to free himself: an arm
had got stuck here, a leg there, nose and eyes
cruelly compressed by the twine.

Ramona, for her part, now hardly left the
apartment: almost everything was too much
trouble. She was delighted at Rupinello's new
job at the circus, for it was show business after

all, and akin to the opera, her own particular love. She had always longed to go to the circus, but now that she had the chance she wouldn't go. She didn't want people to see her so swollen, and besides, she had outgrown her clothes. She contented herself instead with Rupinello's stories of circus life, and listened wide-eyed to his tales of the clowns, the bearded lady, the acrobats and the lion tamer.

Ramona now lived to eat. Immediately on opening her pink eyes, which had sunk still further into the folds of her pink cheeks, her first thought was of food. Her arms seemed to have shortened as her pregnancy advanced, and so Rupinello had furnished her with a stick with which to beat on the wall to get his attention.

'Rupinello, breakfast!' she would cry, then, with increasing urgency, 'Breakfast!' And Rupinello, who already had the tray waiting, fully prepared, would hurry in. There would be fresh morning rolls, baby cakes, honey, a good-sized sausage, ham or brawn, eggs which Rupinello would soft boil in his little kettle, buffalo mozzarella, and coffee. Sometimes, if business the day before had been brisk, there would be the little paper cone of chocolates that Ramona loved more than anything else.

Once Ramona had vacuumed all the crumbs from the tray she would allow Rupinello into bed with her, his reward for bringing the breakfast. Rinaldo would already have left the apartment. Ramona never bothered to ask where he went. It was enough for her that he went out early in the morning and did not return until late at night. What he did during that time she didn't much care.

And so Rupinello would nestle down next to the child swelling inside her, nourished by the fruits of his labours, while she stroked the hump to bring herself the good luck he sold to others. He had already come to regard the baby as his own. If Santa Margherita had been listening to his prayers, the baby would be born like him with a miniature hump, uneven legs and a knobby face.

As he lay near her, inhaling her scent, he thought how life would have been without the hump. If he had been born with a body as straight and strong as an oak tree. Then love would not have been denied him. It would have been his right, as it is with every other person. Then Ramona would have loved him, as she had once loved Rinaldo. Yes, she would have felt the passion for him that a woman can feel for a well-formed man; she can only feel pity for a humpback.

All too soon he would have to leave to begin his heavy day's work, and the glowing intimacy of the early morning would come to an end. Rupinello was then obliged to hurry to secure his pitch on the Strada di Toledo and ply his hump whilst Ramona's sensuous touch was still warm upon it. How he wished he could bottle her touch and keep it with him, and uncork it every so often throughout the day to keep her near him. How he resented the first customer of the day who, through no fault of his own, dispersed the magic of Ramona's caress and left him with nothing but the dull brush of mortal fingers.

CHAPTER NINETEEN

AN ERUPTION OF THE VOLCANO

One night Ramona was savouring dreams of veal pies piled high on huge platters, suckling pigs roasting on spits, bottled fruits. One by one, in a long procession, the kitchen men and maids from La Casa appeared. They passed by her bearing salvers loaded with everything from antipasti to zabaglione. Immacolata Pescatore stood at Ramona's side and instead of smacking her hands away from the tasty morsels, as she had done in real life, she smiled at her and said, 'Eat whatever pleases Your Ladyship.'

Ramona needed little encouragement. In her sleep she was salivating. A trickle of juices trailed across her cheek, seeped into the upturned tulip of her ear and wet her white hair before forming a swampy mess on the pillow.

On the other side of the grubby mattress lay the unwanted husband, Rinaldo. It was not for him to enjoy the sweet dreams of laden platters, the roasted flesh and rubbery eels. Although his dream world returned him to the estate, it was not to the plentiful kitchens, but to the dismal cottage in the orchard.

In Rinaldo's dream a baby girl was born, and she was the image of her mother, with white fairy hair and pink cheeks and eyes. The baby brought joy back to the lives of Rinaldo and Ramona. Now they were a real family.

In the confused perspective of the dream, the cottage had been transplanted to the city and was sitting amongst the hovels and ugliness and filth of the Via Vecchia Poggioreale. As they played with the baby, the cottage door opened and all that had been light became suddenly dark. A figure entered.

Against the light it was not possible to make out who it was. But then his eyes focused and Rinaldo saw the beekeeper. The beekeeper was more horribly decomposed than Rinaldo had seen him in his other dreams. The flesh was dripping from his face like falling rain. His empty eye sockets turned towards the baby and he reached out his skeletal hands to her. Rinaldo leapt in front of the crib to shield his daughter, but the beekeeper did not stop. He kept coming closer and closer.

'Stay back!' screamed Rinaldo, holding out his arms to repel the beekeeper's approach.

'Keep away from her. Stay back.'

'I have come to claim a life in payment for my own which you took,' said the beekeeper, reaching out his hands towards the baby gurgling in the crib.

'No!' screamed Rinaldo. 'No!'

But still the beekeeper kept coming. Rinaldo could not hold him back. There was no strength in his arms. They had become soft like rubber. Rinaldo started up from the bed in a raging fever with his eyes wide open. Though he was still asleep, he ran into the kitchen and seized a knife. Ramona, awakened abruptly from her feast of a dream, felt in the darkness for her stick and thumped on the wall for Rupinello to come and help. Rupinello naturally thought she wanted food, and rushed to the cook shop. When he reappeared bearing a *pentola* of *costine* in his arms, Rinaldo was edging and prancing around the apartment, making parrying attacks with the knife.

'Take that,' he shouted with a bayoneting action which made a hole in the wall. Plaster trickled from other holes onto the floor, and in places the knife had cut right through the wall so the night sky could be seen in the fissures, black with a sprinkling of stars.

Ramona hauled herself out of the bed she had not left in weeks and took refuge behind the upturned table from where she peered out like an inflated mouse.

'You humpbacked fool!' she screamed. 'I

didn't want food, I needed help. You've been gone for ages. I could have been murdered.'

Chastened, Rupinello set down the cooking pot and began to circle Rinaldo, trying to disarm him without any spilling of blood.

'*Attento!*' cried Rinaldo, lunging at Rupinello. With a deft movement learned in the circus ring, the humpback flung himself between Rinaldo's open legs and somersaulted back onto his feet. The knife lodged in the upturned tabletop where it quivered with the force of the blow.

'Ramona!' screamed Rupinello, fearing for his love's safety behind the flimsy piece of furniture. There was no sound. Had she been punctured by the blow? Why didn't she speak? Rupinello ran to the spot, mad with terror and rage. The space behind the table was empty. Ramona had disappeared. What could this mean? Swinging himself around in a panic, Rupinello let out a roar like a lioness when her cubs are threatened, a roar which made the Castorellis start up from their beds fearing an eruption of the volcano.

In haste they gathered the bags of money secreted in the apartment, and loaded them into the barrow acquired for this very purpose. Outside in the street, however, all was quiet. There were no crowds fleeing with their belongings, loading their mules and carts with everything of value: bedding and kettles, furniture and grandmothers. No, their

130

neighbours slept on with the peace of angels. The night sky over to the east in the direction of the volcano was not illuminated. No sulphurous clouds hung in the air. No ashes rained down on the rooftops. No, the commotion was not coming from the fire-breathing mountain. It was coming from the top floor apartment in their own building.

Nonna Pino was terribly confused. She thought she recognized one of the stockings on her son-in-law's barrow. Could it be that her worst fears were confirmed, that the fiend who had made off with her portion was her own son-in-law?

Having secured their treasure, the Castorellis raced up to their tenants' rooms. Ramona had only been saved by a miracle. The pot of ribs caused her to abandon the place of apparent safety and crawl along the floor to secure the tasty contents of the *pentola*. While the fight was at its peak she sat in the far corner of the room, sucking the flesh from the bones and mopping up the sauce from the dish with her tongue.

The Castorellis watched in astonishment as Rupinello wrestled with Rinaldo to maintain control of the knife he had pulled from the table. The humpback was on top, straddling the giant. It was no longer simply a contest over the knife: Rupinello was fighting a battle for life. For the pain and misery of his deformity, for his jealousy, his unrequited love, his hopelessness. He would fight on even if it killed him.

Ramona, having done justice to the pork ribs, was licking the last traces of the sauce from her face. She was watching the struggle in a detached way, and did not seem to care which of the combatants came out the victor.

The Castorellis, however, were clear in their support for the humpback.

'Kill him, Rupinello!' screamed Amalasunta. 'Drive the knife into his neck.'

Her husband, frustrated by his lack of speech, flapped his arms like a great bird while making monkey faces with his lips. He then made the mistake of groping at Ramona where she lay on the floor, straddling her bulge with legs apart. With a motion he could not have anticipated she gripped the offending hand between her teeth and clenched down on it, severing the tendons and veins, which caused the blood to spurt upwards like a fountain.

Signor Castorelli was unable to scream, so nobody took any notice of him. At that point Nonna Pino staggered into the apartment. She had searched her daughter's rooms but found no trace of her treasure. Exhausted by rage and by the flights of steps, she seemed on the brink of death.

'A curse on you, Amando Castorelli,' she muttered as she fell down on top of Rupinello and Rinaldo who were still engaged in the frenzied combat. The form of Nonna Pino falling onto them succeeded in breaking up the fight where all else had failed. Rinaldo woke up and no longer believed he was fighting with the beekeeper. Rupinello rolled onto his back on the floor where he lay, his tiny chest heaving with the sustained effort he had made.

Nonna Pino now became the focus of attention as she lay back on the floor beside Rupinello, also gasping for breath. Amalasunta was bending over her mother as her husband bound his hand with a filthy rag he had found in the sink.

'A curse on you Amando Castorelli,' she repeated in a hoarse voice, 'I saw my stocking of gold on your barrow.' Here she broke off, struggling for the breath to complete her dying curse.

'Come now, Mother,' Amalasunta filled the gap. 'Now is not the time for making curses. It is the time for making your peace with God.'

'I curse him,' gasped Nonna Pino with her final dregs of life, fixing her bleeding son-in-law with a look full of hate. 'He took my gold, my life savings. Thief, I curse you. You will die an agonizing death, you will pay the price of your treachery. Death to him. Death. Death . . .' With that, and without having the time to complete her curse, Nonna Pino's head fell to one side and her eyes assumed the glaze of death.

Amalasunta caught her mother's final breath in her lips and then closed her eyes with her fingers. No more would Nonna Pino bring joy to all who knew her. No more would she offer her delightful observations on life to passers-by in the Via Vecchia Poggioreale. Amalasunta could not help but shed a tear.

What a night it had been. What a scene of devastation was there in the lovers' apartment. While Nonna Pino lay dying, Rinaldo had wandered off to bed where he now lay snoring soundly, exhausted by the fight with Rupinello, but otherwise apparently unscathed. Rupinello lay on the floor next to the corpse. His strength was gone and he was shaking uncontrollably. He was never to recover fully from the events of that terrible night.

Ramona was also lying on the floor, watching. Her appetite had been inflamed by the excitement and the sight and taste of blood and she was waiting with impatience for Rupinello to recover sufficiently to make the journey to the cook shop. Tripe was what her heart then craved above all else. Tripe stewed with beans, pancetta and *parmigiano*. And a hunk of crusty bread with which to soak up the juices.

Signor Castorelli was unable to stem the flow of blood from his wound. It poured to the floor in a steady stream, and he had lost all sensation in the hand which had been the subject of Ramona's attack. He was in a bad way but did his best to help his wife carry the corpse of Nonna Pino down the steps.

From being a strong, vibrant man in the peak of condition, Signor Castorelli was rapidly reduced by blood poisoning to a shrunken and sunken wretch that bore no resemblance to his former self. Amalasunta herself soon found it difficult to recognize him. Yet it never occurred to her to call a doctor. Even when Amando lost his tongue in the accident, they had coped alone. Amando had healed himself. The blood loss was worse then than it was now. Her Amando certainly knew how to bleed. They had kept the tongue for some time in a jar of vinegar on the washstand in case some good use could be discovered for it, but there being none, they fed it to a mongrel hound that made its home in the street. They never had liked to see anything going to waste, and although they could not bring themselves to make a meal of it, the dog was glad of it.

Alas, there could be no touching last words to his tender-hearted wife. Nor were there even any last gestures of love, for Signor Castorelli was delirious to the end. His passing was marked by nothing more than a final trembling that suddenly became still, and Amalasunta knew then that he was gone.

One consolation in the face of this double tragedy was that Amalasunta was able to bury husband and mother together in the same plot in the cemetery, thus saving considerably on the cost of two single funerals. It was with a grave sense of satisfaction that she ordered an extra-large coffin from the undertakers in the Via Casanova, and when it was delivered she squeezed both the corpses inside, top to tail. To be sure there was something of an overlap; the squashing up of a leg here, an arm there. But she felt confident that her husband would approve the move, saving as it did some twenty scudi in total, and reasoned that her mother was too far gone now to care.

And so the son-in-law and the mother-in-law made curious bedfellows beneath the earth. Nonna Pino continued to utter her curses, to which Amando, his arms restricted by the lack of space, could only respond with contortions of his rubbery face.

CHAPTER TWENTY

A CASE OF MISTAKEN IDENTITY

While the joint funeral was taking place at the Chiesa di Santa Maria del Fede, Rinaldo was wandering the streets aimlessly. As he turned from the Via Torino into the Piazza Garibaldi he saw a figure crossing the street in front of him. He recognized the form immediately, instinctively. The height, the build, the bearing. The sick paralysis of fear gripped him in the stomach. Was there never to be an end to this persecution?

Yes, it was the beekeeper again, now just ahead of him on the pavement. His appurtenances made him particularly noticeable in the city: the protective face mask, the smock, the gauntlets, the gaiters. Around him a swarm of bees buzzed and circled.

Rinaldo knew he could not let him get away this time. He just couldn't allow the beekeeper to go on tormenting him like this, making his life a living hell. With one swift action he could end it, once and for all. He would kill the beekeeper right now, right here, in the street, in front of witnesses, and then there would be no doubt that he was dead, really dead this time. Then Rinaldo could reclaim his own life.

Rinaldo ran at the beekeeper and threw himself on his back. The beekeeper was so surprised at the attack that he staggered round in a circle trying to figure out what was going on. Unable to support Rinaldo's great weight, he finally fell to the ground with Rinaldo still clinging to him.

Rinaldo assailed the beekeeper with kicks and punches. With his enormous block of a head he thrashed at the beekeeper, knocking the sense out of him. Even when the beekeeper lay unconscious, his skull broken into halves like a cracked walnut shell, even then Rinaldo would not give up. The swarm of bees buzzed round and Rinaldo paused only to wave them from his face. He kicked and kicked again at the insensible body, rupturing the internal organs in his fury, punishing the beekeeper for every nightmare of his life.

Even when Rinaldo was pulled away and restrained by three officers of the *carabinieri*, he did not stop thrashing with his arms and legs. It truly was unfortunate that one of the officers received a cut lip which bled on his pristine uniform, and another suffered a black eye and a crushed cap.

'Let me kill him,' he cried. 'Let me kill him finally this time, so he can no longer walk the earth.'

As the onlookers tended to the injured beekeeper, he transformed himself into another man before Rinaldo's very eyes. An old man, with a different face, different hair, different everything. Even the mask and gauntlets had gone, replaced with an ordinary fedora and kid gloves.

'Oh cunning beekeeper!' shrieked Rinaldo, who was accustomed to his tricks. 'You think that by changing form you can cheat me. But you can't. I know you. You are the very devil, changing guises as a mortal man changes his clothes.'

The broken body of the old man released a horrible gurgle.

'His antics would be enough to drive anyone out of their wits,' Rinaldo continued. 'But not me. I'm made of stronger stuff. I'm as sane as ever I was.'

138

Rinaldo was still shouting as the officers dragged him away to the *manicomio* at San Chiara. The injured man, it transpired, was not the beekeeper at all. Rinaldo had made a terrrible mistake. Close to death, he was taken away to the infirmary, where the nuns were appalled at the extent of his injuries. Without delay they gathered the injured man's family around him, and while the priest anointed his wounds with oil, his weeping sons Nabore, Valdo and Oddo swore that their father would be avenged.

CHAPTER TWENTY-ONE

THE HUMPBACK IN HEAVEN

When Ramona heard from two government officials that Rinaldo had been hanged, she greeted the news that she was a widow again with the same relief she had felt the first time around.

Rupinello, naturally, was delighted. That evening when he returned from his act at the circus, he decided to seize his opportunity. He had taken pains to secure a particularly plentiful supper for Ramona. There was a veritable mountain of *spaghetti vongole*, followed by meatballs stuffed with eggs, cheese, sultanas and pine nuts, and to finish,

Rupinello had acquired what Ramona loved most, a paper packet filled with chocolates.

As she gorged he talked.

'Ramona, I don't want to worry you, but our situation is very bad.'

She looked round-eyed at him while continuing to suck the straws of spaghetti into her mouth.

'In fact, it's terrible. Signora Castorelli was going to call the police about the circumstances of her husband's death, so I had to pay her all my savings to buy her silence. I have nothing left.'

He paused and watched as Ramona who had quickly finished the spaghetti now slurped up the few clams that remained at the bottom of the dish.

'And so we need to think of ways we can economize, or otherwise . . .' Rupinello let the words trail away. Then, with perfect timing, he cunningly raised the lid on the *pentola* of meatballs. Once released their wonderful aroma filled the air with its promise of meaty succulence. Juicy little beauties. With a cruel stroke, Rupinello replaced the lid on the pan and continued with his rhetoric.

'As a final extravagance, Ramona, before the meagre days of hunger bite into us, I have managed to get you a little treat.'

Ramona's pink eyes welled with tears at the prospect of hunger.

'Yes,' continued the humpback, pressing

home his advantage, 'chocolates. The very last chocolates we are likely to have.'

Ramona sniffed hard. No more chocolates. Ever.

Thus Rupinello was able to convince Ramona that he would have to move in with her in order to economize, and he lost no time in doing so. On the very first evening of occupation he managed to wheedle his way into Ramona's bed. Naturally, given her condition and her complete lack of all romantic feeling towards him, nothing of love transpired between them. Still, Rupinello enjoyed sharing the bed of a woman for the first time in his life. He resolved that following the birth, their relationship would not remain unconsummated for long. He would have her, he swore, by the grace of San Gennaro himself.

CHAPTER TWENTY-TWO

THE NEW ARRIVAL

Soon after this, Ramona gave birth to the baby. She felt the initial pains early in the morning. At first she thought they were hunger pangs and began to eat the lunch Rupinello had left for her.

She unpacked the basket and set her teeth to the blood sausage and the huge loaf of white bread. Despite this ample nourishment, the pains continued and Ramona began to think she must be ill. Could it be that the sausage was bad? If Rupinello had brought her bad sausage there would be trouble that night when he returned from the circus. Perhaps she was suffering from indigestion. Perhaps she was still hungry.

Then she realized with terror that these pains could signal the onset of the birth. For the first time she missed Rinaldo and wished he was there to help her. How would she manage alone? A while ago Rupinello had spoken of engaging a midwife, but Ramona was then convinced that the birth was still a way off, and so they had done nothing.

Ramona's upbringing in the convent had not prepared her for anything like this. She knew nothing about birth, and did not know what to do or what to expect. Amidst her fearful musings she was shocked to feel a sudden gush of warm water pouring out of her. She felt like a burst pipe. The water was perfumed by her smell, and soon the whole room was filled with her scent now amplified a thousand times.

Spasms seized hold of her, squeezing her mercilessly like an udder at milking time. Ramona began to scream. It was as though her whole body had been taken over by mischievous forces. Ramona called for help but no-one heard her. Or if they did they

142

ignored her. Remarkably the Via Vecchia Poggioreale was empty.

Rupinello was plying his trade in the centre of town. From there he would be heading straight out to the Capodimonte to perform in the matinee at the circus. He might not even return between the matinee and the evening performance if any other work came his way. Stupid humpback, never there when needed.

Ramona writhed in agony all day and into the night. She felt herself being ripped apart. The pain was unbearable. She thought she was sure to die. Where was Rupinello? Why did he not come?

She must have lost consciousness and when she came to her senses Rupinello was mopping her face with a wet cloth. The pain had gone and she found, to her astonishment, that while she was sleeping she had been delivered of a baby girl.

Tears welled in Rupinello's eyes as he handed the infant to her mother. The baby was a miniature duplicate of Ramona. Just like her mother she had candy pink skin and eyes and she had white hair too, but it was unusually long for a baby. She was really quite a fairy. Rupinello's selfish prayers that she should resemble him had not been answered. Santa Margherita had plugs of wax in her ears. There was no trace of Rinaldo about her either. It was as though Ramona had created the baby all by herself.

Ramona immediately fell asleep, she was so exhausted, leaving Rupinello to deal with the baby as best he could. But he too was worn out. The firing of the cannon was taking such a toll on his bruised and broken body. Now there was one more mouth to feed, and if the baby's appetite was anything like her mother's, the outlook was bleak. If only they could run away together: he, Ramona, and the baby. They could forget the debts and begin a new life somewhere else. Somewhere in the country, perhaps. It would be a better place to bring up a child. Perhaps he could take on a smallholding, become a farmer. Ramona might even help him.

While Rupinello lay thinking, becoming more and more enthusiastic about the rural idyll his mind planted for him, he noticed something curious. For the first time Ramona's scent was not hanging heavy in the air. Odd. There was no smell except the usual odour of the rooms: dampness and decay. These and the neighbourhood smells of open sewers and filth had until this moment been masked by Ramona's magical fragrance. Now all the disgusting smells crowded at once into Rupinello's nostrils, vying with one another for space. He felt quite sick as a result and was forced to cover his nose with his sleeve. What had happened to Ramona's smell, the smell he loved and cherished above all else? Where had it gone?

CHAPTER TWENTY-THREE

THE SMELL VANISHES

Throughout that sleepless night Rupinello could smell the blood and bones from the abattoir. He could smell Amalasunta Castorelli's feet, two floors below. He could smell the rat droppings in the passage. He could smell the stale pipe tobacco of Signor Scarpetta who lived across the street.

Without Ramona's scent he felt naked, a stranger alone in a foreign land.

In the faint glimmer of light he looked at Ramona sleeping soundly. He sniffed her like a dog, straining to recover some trace of the perfume. He sniffed at the nape of her neck, as it nestled into the pillow. He sniffed her matted hair. He raised the bedclothes and sniffed underneath them. Here the scent would gather in an aura close to her sleeping form; here it was always strongest. He raised her nightgown and sniffed at the folds of skin between her legs, her swollen belly, the space between her breasts. There was no trace of the maddening elixir that had held him captive these past months.

Rupinello spent the night watching and waiting for the smell to return. It had to come back. Please let it come back. He could not bear to be without it. How could it just disappear? Where had it gone? He would look for it and he would find it. He would follow it anywhere.

In the hour before dawn, the hour of clarity when our true selves are illuminated and we recognize our own secret truths, he realized he did not love Ramona. More than that, he now knew he had never loved her. Now the smell had been stripped away he saw her for the first time as she really was and he was repulsed by her. Her livid pink face with its clumsy features, the way her mouth gaped in sleep exuding a frothy mess onto the pillow. He looked with horror at her ugly nostrils. How could he have imagined he loved those? Now he almost hated her. How could he have deluded himself so?

He felt like such a fool. And a fool without a single *carlino* to his name. He owed several weeks' protection money and now watched constantly over his shoulder, fearing that one silent night he would feel a stiletto piercing his hump. The cook shop which had, up to now, provided Ramona's meals, had also threatened him with violence: he had until the week's end to settle his account. Only yesterday, in a warning gesture, the patron, Selmo Filangieri, had sent him a pig's ear on a plate, garnished with parsley and a sauce of capers. His own ears now stung with fear. There would be no more food until he found the money. How

146

could he continue to feed her? She had become a giant mouth and stomach feeding upon him.

Amalasunta Castorelli, that merry widow, held her hand outstretched every time she saw him. Now her very feet were inside his nose. He could not keep paying. It would all have to stop. His head spun. What could he do? How could he free himself? The loathsome smells crowded his nasal passages. He could hardly breathe. Air. He needed air. He had to get away from the stench of this place. He had to think. Quietly he rose and went outside, leaving Ramona and the baby sleeping. He would head towards the Capodimonte. The air was fresher there. He would walk in the pinewoods and think.

Some time later, when Ramona had recovered her strength, she too decided to take a breath of air outside. A little walk in the street. She had not left the apartment in months and she felt a desire to stretch her legs. Yet when she emerged from the house, leaving the baby upstairs, something strange happened: a chimney sweep walked straight past her without even raising his eyes from the ground. Bad sinuses, she thought.

Then a band of three or four oystercatchers went by on their way to the docks. Not one of them bothered to sniff the air. How odd. Fishermen were usually the first to detect her scent, their sense of smell sharpened by the

147

odour of the briny sea. Then a butcher's boy rode past on his bicycle. He whistled away without giving her a glance. Then a troop of foot soldiers marched past without even breaking file. What was going on? Surely all these men did not have blocked noses?

Ramona walked a little further. She deliberately stepped in the path of a passing archdeacon, but he stepped smartly around her and went on his way without even a cursory bulging of the surplice. And so it went on. With all the traffic on the Via Vecchia Poggioreale that day, the acrobats, plasterers, glow-worm trainers, pancake men, and policemen who always gathered round her and followed her to her destination, not a single person noticed her. It was as though Ramona Drottoveo did not even exist.

It felt strange not to be jostled by crowds. Not to be accosted by pleas and prayers and heckles. She felt suddenly small and scared and insignificant. What had happened to her?

Ramona returned to her rooms and was almost surprised to see the baby on the bed. She had completely forgotten about it. She picked it up and grappled with it. The baby struggled in her arms and seemed reluctant to be held. It was very heavy, and it was bigger than she remembered. Not that Ramona cared; she was preoccupied with the fear of having become ordinary. Where was her scent? Perhaps it was exhausted by the birth and was simply renewing itself, ready to burst forth in a few days with even more potency.

She waited impatiently for Rupinello to come. She was miserable and hungry. Where was the humpback? Why did he not bring a pizza or a *frittata*?

What Ramona did not know as she waited and waited, growing more and more hungry, was that Rupinello, her little servant, was not coming back. That night when he sat waiting for the smell to recover was a turning point in his life. As Ramona paced the floor in hunger, Rupinello was on the road to Roma with his new love, the bearded lady from the circus, Monalda Spantigati. Lured on by the scent of the hormonal imbalance that caused her follicles to spout their rich growth of umber bristles, the humpback had agreed to take an engagement at Vanvitelli's circus in the capital.

Thus, at a stroke, he left behind the huge edifice of burdens he had constructed for himself on the foundations of a false and foolish love. The hungry mouths, the outstretched palms, the Camorra, the cook shop, Amalasunta Castorelli. They could go to hell, for all he cared. He was free. Free! With what joy did he skip along the highway, holding the hand of his hairy friend! He blessed the fates for their timely intervention, for his escape from the hungry jaws that were about to swallow him whole. He would not be so foolish again. He had learned his lesson. He

knew better now than to allow himself to be
led by his nose.

CHAPTER TWENTY-FOUR

TO THE CIRCUS

Soon Ramona Drottoveo was knawing on her
fingers. She could not understand where the
humpback had gone. He should have been
back long ago. She had gone all day without
food. He had not even left her a basket for her
breakfast or lunch. What could he be thinking
of? There would be trouble when he did finally
roll in, his sooty face gaping, craving a kiss.
Well there would be no kiss for him this
evening. He must be punished.

In desperation, she decided she could wait
no longer: she would have to find something to
eat on her own. She scraped together the few
grains that she had managed to keep hidden
from Rinaldo and Rupinello and hurried out
to the grocer's on the corner of the Via
Arenaccia. Her little money did not buy much,
only a small loaf and a morsel of cheese, and
once back in her rooms she hurriedly
swallowed what there was, and was still
hungry. Oh, what she would do for ravioli or a
fluffy beef and onion pie.

The night passed and when Ramona awoke

early the next morning Rupinello had still not returned. She glanced at the baby. Overnight it had doubled in size, like rising dough. It seemed strange, but she had no experience with babies. How could she know what to expect? She decided to go to the circus and make enquiries about Rupinello. Maybe he had been injured in an accident. If he had been taken to the infirmary, she would visit him there. He was sure to have some money which would keep her until he could resume his act. He should not lie idle for too long, it wouldn't be good for him.

And so Ramona got ready and set out on the long journey to Capodimonte. It was a beautiful day. Had she not been so hungry and had the baby not been so big and heavy to carry and had it not been so far it would have been quite a pleasant walk. As she made her way along, she looked over her shoulder to see whether anyone followed her, but there were no amorous crowds of scullions and courtiers. In the Via Casanova she passed eleven wandering minstrels, two puppeteers, three taxidermists and twenty-seven civil servants. Not one of them joined step with her. Not one sniffed. Not one made a lewd remark. It did seem as though her worst fears were confirmed. The smell had deserted her. She was no longer special.

What a long walk it was to the circus. To think Rupinello did this walk twice every day.

151

Sometimes four times. It was not surprising that he was always tired. She would tell him to get her a perambulator: the baby was too heavy to carry around. At last the big top loomed huge in the distance. As Ramona approached she saw the clowns, the tumblers, the fire-eaters practising their acts out of doors in the sunshine.

She could not see Rupinello. It was plain he had been injured as she suspected. She felt that the Donadio Brothers should at the very least have sent someone round with a hamper of food and some money. Magnanimously she decided to absolve Rupinello of the greater measure of blame. The patrons were responsible.

A strongman walked past in a loincloth of lion skin.

'Where is Rupinello? What has happened to him?' she asked as he spat on his palms and prepared to begin his training with a number of leaden dumb-bells.

'I haven't seen him, lady. Ask the ringmaster.' He pointed in the direction of a smaller tent at some little distance from the big top. So Rupinello had got this young woman into trouble. Not surprising then that he had fled. Let the ringmaster tell her. The Great Massimo wasn't about to involve himself in that pretty mess. Heave ho.

Ramona hurried over to the tent, preparing to tell the ringmaster just what she thought of him.

'But my dear signora,' replied the mustachioed Signor Donadio when Ramona broke off from her complaint long enough to catch her breath. 'There has been some misunderstanding. Rupinello has not been maimed in an accident. In truth he has run away owing me money. Monalda Spantigati too has disappeared. The word is that they have gone to Roma, to the circus of that lizard, Vanvitelli. To think, she had no beard when I discovered her selling matches in the Via Mezzocannone. I brought her up. I drew out her whiskers. Never have I seen such whiskers on a woman. What a fine bristly growth! And this is how she repays me. What ingratitude. Why I fairly boil to think about it! She and the humpback. Who would have thought it? And so now I have two openings. I have no-one to fire from the canon, and no bearded lady. Now, how will I draw the crowds? I will lose money. The punters will drift away to that villain Corenzio. It is said he has two women with bristles. Twins. But they cannot be genuine . . .'

Ramona had turned and walked away. She did not want to hear any more. The ringmaster's talk was making her head spin.

'Hey, signora, I don't suppose you have any bristles, do you? Any sprouting warts or moles? I can help you. I can draw out your natural talents. You would look amazing with a

153

beard. Your colouring is so unusual. A pink woman with a white beard. Think about it. What a draw for the crowds. We would be packing them in. Standing room only. All I ask is that you think about it, signora . . .'

Ramona left the tent. One phrase stuck in her mind. The humpback had gone. That much she understood. Now what would she do? How would she survive?

Hours later, Ramona found herself back at the Via Vecchia Poggioreale, although she was not conscious of having walked there. As she opened the door she thought of Amalasunta Castorelli. Amalasunta Castorelli could help her. She was a wealthy woman now. Why, had they not always been on the best of terms? They were more like friends than landlady and tenant. No, more than friends, sisters. Amalasunta would not see her starve.

CHAPTER TWENTY-FIVE

SWEET CHARITY

Ramona put the baby down on the stairs and knocked on the door of Amalasunta's rooms. There were scrabbling noises within. Rats, of course. The abattoir attracts them. Some of them as big as dogs. She shuddered. Still Amalasunta did not come to the door. She would let herself in: they didn't stand on ceremony with one another.

Ramona admitted herself into the parlour. It was like a warehouse; every surface was covered with piles of goods: miniature glass bottles, wax dolls dressed as priests, and boxes packed with what looked like blackened sausages. They did not look appetizing but Ramona was starving so she stuffed three all at once into her mouth. Uuurrhh. They were not sausages at all. They contained sawdust, not meat. Ramona spat them out in disgust. Surely Amalasunta couldn't have grown rich selling such inedible sausages?'

'There's someone there, I tell you,' came the worried voice of a man Ramona didn't recognize.

'There's no-one there. It's only the rats,' came the voice of Amalasunta, sounding strangely honeyed. 'You should see the size of the rats we get in this district. Huge.'

'Someone has let himself in, I tell you,' came the man's voice again, this time accompanied by the fumbling noise of someone climbing hurriedly into his clothes. 'He's in the parlour.'

Strange. Whose could that voice be.

'There's no-one there, my prince, come back to bed.'

So Amalasunta had a prince in there! Ramona quickly adjusted her hair. Here was her chance to make an impression. If she could

155

get in with a prince her worries would be over. If only her smell had not deserted her she would snatch him from Amalasunta's grasp.

Ramona assumed her most seductive pose on top of one of the crates. But it was not a prince who emerged from Amalasunta Castorelli's bedchamber. It was a young priest with a red face under the biretta he was hurrying to cram onto his head. His vestments were in a state of disarray, and as he ran from the front door, trying to assume an air of composure he could not feel, he was still seeking to adjust them.

Then Amalasunta emerged, she too struggling to put on clothes. Her honeyed tone had evaporated and Ramona could tell her interruption was not welcome.

'What do you mean, bursting in here when I am taking my spiritual guidance?' she demanded.

'I'm sorry,' said Ramona, 'but I'm hungry. I thought you might have a little of your offal stew to spare.'

'Offal stew indeed! The nerve! No, I haven't got any offal stew to spare. I haven't got anything to spare. Now get out.'

'But Amalasunta Castorelli, I need to talk to you. Rupinello has gone.'

'So he's finally seen the light, has he? Well, good for him. So how are you going to pay the rent?'

'That's what I wanted to talk to you about.

Seeing that you and I have always been such good friends, I . . .'

'Friends indeed! Your rent's due Friday. Pay up or you'll be on the street. Now get out.' With that Amalasunta opened the door and bundled her friend, her sister, Ramona out into the stinking passage.

So much for charity.

CHAPTER TWENTY-SIX

'NEVER SEEN HER BEFORE, BUBBONE'

Who else could Ramona ask for help? There was, of course, Signor Po at the opera house. Although he had never summoned her to take the stage, if he knew her circumstances he would be sure to help her. He wouldn't allow her to starve, not after all they had been to one another. There was also the gentleman who had taken her to the Fontana Refreshment Rooms. What was his name now? It was Signor Pastini, she was sure of it. She scrabbled about in a drawer and came up with his card. It was torn and stained but it would allow her to find him.

'It's a good thing I am so clever,' Ramona said to the baby which had grown even more during the night. 'I will save us. Now we must go out again, and this time we won't return hungry.'

And so Ramona strapped on her eyeglasses and set off to the San Carlo. Instead of the beautiful clothes of Brunella Tosti she was dressed now in her own dowdy rags, but she hoped Signor Po wouldn't notice the difference. She hurried across town with the enormous baby in her arms, hoping she would soon be sitting down to a lavish meal. She staggered up the steps of the opera house and made her way into the vestibule. There was a different concierge this time, not the friendly man who had escorted her to Signor Po's office. The former concierge had been relieved of his duties. He was still in prison awaiting execution for the brutal murder of his wife.

'The house is closed, signora,' the new concierge informed her.

'I wish to see Signor Po,' said Ramona.

'Signor Po is no longer with the San Carlo, signora.'

'No longer here?' Ramona panicked. 'But I must see him.'

'Sorry, he's gone. Difference of opinion with the management. Can't help you. Good day.' With that he ushered Ramona out onto the steps and quickly closed the door.

The concierge nodded slyly to Panfilo, the deaf caretaker, who was then passing by with a mop. 'Just had another of Signor Po's *bastardi* in, Panfilo,' he bellowed. 'That makes three already this week.'

The caretaker shrugged. What did he care about Signor Po's *bastardi*? He had worries enough of his own.

So much for Signor Po. With her little remaining strength Ramona decided to approach Signor Pastini and try her luck with him. He was her final hope. She asked a passer-by to direct her to the address on the card and made her way to the house in the Piazza Matteotti. She rang the bell at the imposing entrance, and finally her call was answered by an impertinent butler:

'Trade calls round the back,' he sniffed, not deigning to look at her.

'I'm not trade,' replied Ramona angrily. 'I have come to call on Signor Pastini. Kindly tell him I wish to see him.'

'I am sure the signor is not accustomed to receiving persons such as yourself,' he sneered. 'Anyway the signor is not at home.'

'Well please make sure to tell him I called, and will call again tomorrow.'

Without replying the butler shut the door, leaving Ramona and the baby on the doorstep. What was she to do now? There was no-one else to try. Yet as she turned to go, a carriage drew up and Signor Pastini himself stepped out of it. Heavens be praised! Here was her chance. All was not yet lost.

'Signor, do you remember me?' called Ramona, lurching towards him.

159

'I've never seen you before,' the signor replied, eyeing the baby with mistrust.

'But signor, you know you have; we took coffee together at the Fontana. You asked me to go to a hotel with you. You said you would help me. You gave me your card.' She held out the grubby scrap for him to see.

'No, you must be mistaken. I've never seen you before in my life, signora. Good day.'

The signor stepped around her and made for his front door, which was immediately opened by the supercilious butler.

'But Signor,' pleaded Ramona, 'Please . . .'

'Never seen her before, Bubbone,' said the signor to his butler as the latter shut the door on Ramona for the second time.

'Just as I thought, sir,' replied the butler with evident satisfaction.

CHAPTER TWENTY-SEVEN

THE SEDUCTION OF SIGNOR FILANGIERI

Ramona returned to her rooms to find Amalasunta showing them to one of her suitors. The signor was testing the bedsprings with an amorous look in his eye and Ramona heard Amalasunta saying: 'She'll be leaving Friday. You can move your stuff in then.'

160

'I'll be here in time for the siesta,' he replied, sparkling.

'Not so fast,' said Ramona. 'I'll have the money to you by Friday, you can depend upon it.'

Ignoring her, Amalasunta led her admirer down the steps, the two of them making plans for his occupancy of the rooms Ramona had not yet vacated.

Everything had failed her. At last she began to think in earnest about returning to the estate. The Signora would take her back. She would not turn her away. It would be demeaning to admit her failure in the city, but survival came before pride. If she did not return she knew she would die.

But how would she make the journey? She had no money to pay for a place in a coach. She just had to hope she could beg a ride. She would leave tomorrow. She couldn't go now: it was late and she was exhausted. She had to rest.

She regretted now that she hadn't agreed to go back to the estate with Rinaldo. She had been foolish. He was right: Napoli was no place for them. They didn't belong. Here your neighbours would happily watch you starve. That would never happen in the country.

A knock on the door made Ramona jump. In the shadows of the filthy passage a man was lurking: it was Selmo Filangieri, the patron of the cook shop of the same name.

The signor came inside and deposited a huge basket of victuals on the floor. He had just shut up shop and was on his way home, taking with him his family's supper. The aroma of roasted flesh mingled with succulent sauces of garlic, cheese, tomatoes and freshly baked *focaccia*. Ramona was ready to swoon. It really was torture for one in her position.

'The humpback owes me money,' Signor Filangieri growled. 'If he is gone, who will pay?'

'I cannot pay, signor,' said Ramona, 'but I am starving almost to death. Could you give me a little of what you have in your basket? Just some roasted flesh, some bread, some cheese . . .'

'You must think me a fool,' thundered the signor. '"Some roasted flesh, some bread" indeed! I'll give you nothing more, you hear, and I want my money.'

'Perhaps, signor,' said Ramona spying an opportunity through her pink eyes. 'Perhaps we could come to some arrangement.'

Here she came up close to Signor Filangieri, and puffing out her chest she laid her grubby hands upon his intimate parts. There could have been no doubt as to what was running through her mind. The signor was aghast.

'I want my money,' he said in a steel-tipped tone, before throwing Ramona roughly aside, picking up his basket and banging the door shut behind him. As he stamped down the

162

stairs he shouted back: 'You can expect a visit from the debt collectors.'

Debt collectors! How horrible those words sounded to Ramona who lay bruised on the floor.

CHAPTER TWENTY-EIGHT

THE EAGER CLEAVER OF LIBERIO BORRELLI

Amalasunta meanwhile had changed her mind about the allocation of Ramona's rooms. A decision which was to have the most awful consequences. The following morning she called in at the little butcher's shop in the Via Camillo Porzio to tell Liberio Borrelli that he couldn't have her lodgings after all. Last night over supper with Rambaldo Melandri the crib-maker, she had decided that Rambaldo was in and Liberio was out.

Liberio finished slicing the fillet of pork then under his knife and wiped his hands on his bloodstained apron. He was distraught but kept his feelings to himself. In truth it was the Widow Castorelli he was interested in, not the rooms; and more than that, it was the gold, not the widow, that was the ultimate object of his desires. In his mind he pictured the spacious premises that drove him ever onward. The double frontage. The gleaming white tiles. The fashionable clientele. He watched Amalasunta go, and then followed her at a safe distance.

Meanwhile Ramona was getting ready to leave the city. She had no possessions to speak of. Nothing to pack. But she had to have some food inside her in order to make the journey. How could she get it? She would rob Amalasunta, of course! Why hadn't she thought of it before? She left the great baby in the passage and let herself into the ground floor apartment.

Soon the creak of the bedsprings and the low moans of love alerted Ramona to the presence of the landlady and her companion, and she began her search without fear. The parlour piled high with bizarre merchandise yielded nothing. Similarly the kitchen. She looked in all the obvious places: the coffee pot, the salt cellar, the waste bucket. Nothing.

There was not even any food in the cupboards, only the unwashed pots and plates from last night's stew piled high on the drainer, and Amalasunta was so mean that even these had been scraped almost bare. Still, the filmy aftermath of gravy constituted a meal to one in the advanced stages of malnutrition: Ramona licked everything clean. Despite the dangers, she knew she had to try the bedroom.

Fortunately for Ramona, Amalasunta and her exuberant priest were going at it hammer and tongs, blissfully unaware of the thief in their midst. Ramona checked the bedpan, the closet, the pockets of the hurriedly discarded clothing; all she found were a couple of grains in the shoe of the clergyman. It would have to do. She knew there had to be millions secreted here, but she couldn't risk discovery by prolonging her search.

Ramona tiptoed out of the apartment and ran out into the street. Then she remembered she had left the baby. Without much hesitation she went back inside, snatched it up, and this time made her escape.

Outside, across the street, Liberio Borrelli was watching from a doorway. Here was a man on the brink of an abyss. He had known that there were two dentists ahead of him in Amalasunta's affections, one crib-maker and three assorted civil servants, but he had known nothing of the handsome young priest whom he had seen admitting himself into the house with his very own key a short while before.

He knew he stood no chance in the face of such competition. The years were rolling on and he was not getting any younger. His hair was thinning to the extent that he had to comb over the surviving strands from a parting at the nape of his neck. He knew also that without Amalasunta's gold his dream of the double-fronted premises in fashionable San Giuseppe would remain just that, a dream.

As Liberio Borrelli stood there contemplating a dismal future it started to rain. The glossy drops quickly made a mockery of his tonsorial artifice. The wisps gravitated towards his collar leaving his pate ingloriously exposed. The indignity of it all overwhelmed him.

Seizing his resolve and his eager cleaver he burst in on the lovers and hacked them to death. Then, with the glassy eyes of Amalasunta watching him, from the floor where her head had rolled amongst the muck and dust, he ransacked the apartment. Perhaps those glassy eyes shone with triumph when the butcher could not uncover so much as a single gold piece. The treasure had been hidden where no-one would ever find it.

Finally, in a despair which bordered on madness, Liberio Borrelli fled from the scene of the crime, leaving suspicion to fall on the vanished tenant from the upper floor, the candy-coloured woman whose husband had been a murderer before her: Ramona.

Part Three

THE COUNTRY ONCE MORE

CHAPTER TWENTY-NINE

OUT ON THE HIGHWAY

Ramona bought and swallowed as much bread as her two grains would buy, and then set off on the long journey back to the estate. Raindrops the size of plums penetrated her clothes with indecent precision, and caused her eyeglasses to steam up, but she hardly seemed to notice. She sped through the *Orto Botanico,* sometimes looking back over her shoulder as though afraid of being hunted down. She raced through the districts of Il Moiariello, San Efremo Vecchio and into Ponti Rossi beyond. She relaxed her pace only when she joined the main highway to Aversa and could see the open countryside in the distance.

Occasionally a wagon or cart would pass by and she would hail the driver and ask for a ride. Each took one look at her, twitched the reins, and drove on faster, splattering her with mud. How she hated life without the aroma. In the old days, a convoy of carters would be begging her to ride with them.

Oh, the baby was heavy. It was so much bigger than other babies. And it grew so fast. Although only a few days old, it already looked a year or more. What ill luck, she thought, to have one of such abnormal size. As she carried the baby it grew bigger and heavier still, and Ramona, already weak, grew weaker and weaker.

It was the baby's fault the smell had vanished, and that made Ramona dislike it even more. On this arduous journey, away from the noise and bustle of the city, she was able to think more clearly, and she realized that her bad luck had begun with the baby's unwelcome appearance. The creature weighing so heavily in her arms was now an object of bitter resentment. What a burden it was to one so hungry and tired and wet. How she would like to set it down for a while and rest.

She put the baby down on the verge by the road. It began to scream. What a dreadful noise! Oh, how her arms ached. It would be so good not to have to carry it any more. Not ever again. Suppose she left it here and went on alone?

Alone she would stand a better chance of getting a ride. Yes, it was probably the screeching baby that the carters objected to. Without it, she could have been on a wagon by now, dry and rested. The driver would, of course, share his food with her. A mound of *penne* with beef *ragù* was what her taste buds craved most at that moment. He might even have some cake with him, if she was lucky. He would probably take her right up to the gates of the estate, possibly even inside, to save her the trouble of walking up the long drive.

If she tucked the baby carefully into the ditch it would be safe until someone found it. Someone who wanted a baby, and would take it home and look after it. It wasn't a bad baby really, if you wanted one. Many people, she was sure, would be happy to take it in.

Ramona moved the baby into the ditch. It continued to scream. Then she walked away, stretching out her aching arms and shoulders. She felt so much stronger, not having to lug the extra weight. Now she could concentrate on herself. She had no pangs about leaving the baby. It was simply a matter of survival.

She continued along the road, making better progress. Two carts passed by in quick succession, but neither would take her. One of the drivers threatened her with his whip when she made an attempt to climb on board. It was a good thing she didn't have the baby with her, or it might have been injured.

After travelling alone for an hour or so, Ramona turned around, for some reason, and began to retrace her steps. She didn't understand why her body changed direction, why her legs began to carry her back. Painfully she crept along until she came to the spot where she had left the baby. But the baby was no longer there. Sitting in the ditch was a chubby toddler, with the telltale white hair and rosy flesh. As her mother approached, the child regarded her with a look of pure hatred in her pink eyes. Ramona shuddered. There was something supernatural in the speed with which this child was developing.

'Come with me,' Ramona instructed.

The girl refused to take the hand her mother held out to her. Indeed she recoiled from it. She climbed out of the ditch by herself, and trotted along at Ramona's side. It felt strange to Ramona, but she was relieved she didn't have to carry the child.

The rain poured down relentlessly. Hunger continued to gnaw at her body. Fatigue made her legs so heavy she had to will them to move her forward. Many times she stumbled and fell, covering herself with muck. Each time it grew harder to raise herself to her feet, and as she struggled the girl looked at her viciously, as though willing Ramona to die.

Finally, in the middle of the night, mother and daughter reached the estate. Ramona took hold of the great bell-pull at the front entrance of La Casa, and slumping to the ground with it still in her hand, set off such a clanging of bells that every inhabitant woke with a start.

CHAPTER THIRTY

RAMONA DROTTOVEO IS BACK!

The servants gathered in the great entrance hall trying to account for the calamitous clanging of bells. Could it be the Signora, come back from the dead to haunt them? Or were bandits set to murder them in their beds? Dalinda Scandone, the dull kitchen maid, whose wits had not sharpened over the intervening months, exposed her yellow teeth and began to whinny. She was only silenced by a blow to her head administered by her lover, the potboy, Roberto Pedretti. The newlyweds Immacolata Pescatore and Semprebene Metrofano (yes, they had finally tied the knot) were the last to arrive on the scene, blushing like teenagers under the scrutiny of the gathering.

'Holy Mother, this noise will wake the Signor,' hissed Immacolata. Since the accident that had taken his wife's life and dealt him an almost fatal blow to the head, the Signor had begun to act in curious ways. If he awoke during the night he sometimes crawled around the marble floors of La Casa, sniffing like a bloodhound or, worse still, he invaded the staff quarters and pressed his nose to the forms of the sleeping servants. As a result the entire household was terrified of disturbing him.

'Men, be prepared to defend our lives,' Immacolata continued. 'Now, Ugo Rossi, open the door.'

'Why me?' demanded Ugo, cowering in fear at the rear of the throng. But a barely perceptible narrowing of the head cook's right eye was enough to send him scurrying to undo the bolts. The devil himself was less scary than Immacolata Metrofano in a rage. The other men stood with their fists raised in anticipation of attack while Dalinda Scandone brandished her crucifix and uttered strange imprecations.

When the bolts were thrown back and the great door yawned wide into the night, to the astonishment of the assembly, not a creature was there. No ghost of the Signora. No bristling devils. No body snatchers. No bandits with pitchforks. The bell seemed to be ringing itself. But then Immacolata, who had taken her rightful place at the front, raised a lantern and discovered what looked like a heap of rags at her feet. From the rags a dirty hand emerged, clasping the bell-pull.

Gingerly, Immacolata prised the bell-pull away from the fingers, and then like the sun emerging from behind a cloud after a storm, the terrible clanging finally stopped. Heaven be praised if the din had not penetrated the wax earplugs of the Signor.

But what about the pile of rags? There were fingers in it, that much was evident. Dirty fingers too. Tito Livio Feriani, the Signor's personal valet, stepped forward with the ornamental sword he had snatched up in the heat of the moment. With one neatly executed flourish Tito exposed what lay beneath the tatters, causing the women to release a single scream which rose up above the crowd like a balloon.

Ramona Drottoveo was back!

She was unconscious. Soaked all the way through. But there could be no mistaking the limp figure that lay on the step, with the rubberized goggles strapped to its head.

'It can't be her,' said Ernesto Conticello, the rose gardener, flexing his highly tuned nostrils. 'There's no smell.'

The servants all directed their noses towards the doorstep and inhaled. Ernesto Conticello was right: there was no smell.

'But it must be her,' offered Ugo Rossi tentatively. 'Who else looks like that?'

'So what do we do?' asked Semprebene Metrofano, who was impatient to get back into bed with his bride.

'Let's just shut the door,' said Beata Viola, the silver maid, brightly, 'and maybe by morning she'll have gone.'

'For shame, Beata,' replied Immacolata Metrofano, 'we can't turn her away. For all her faults, and I grant you there are many, she is a human being in need of help. Bring her in, and put her in her old room.'

175

As hands reached out towards Ramona, a child tottered into the circle of light thrown by the lantern. The staff let out a gasp. She was a miniature Ramona. Drenched, but unmistakable. Aged about three or four. How was this possible? Ramona had only been gone six months. How could she have produced a child of such size in that time? The servants exchanged worried looks. It didn't bode well.

CHAPTER THIRTY-ONE

FEVER

Throughout that long night when the maids took turns by the sickbed, it became clear that Ramona was clinging to life by a thread. She hovered near death, and twice seemed actually to die. She stopped breathing and Pupolo Floscio was urgently dispatched to rouse Padre Jacopo from his slumbers. Grumbling, and still wearing the insufficient nightgown which exposed his hairy knees, the priest came to administer the last rites. What a change he found in his former beloved! He was appalled at the feelings he had once harboured in his breast for this repulsive girl.

Yet, both times, when those lurking in the shadows on the back stairs were jubilantly preparing to broadcast to the estate the news of Ramona Drottoveo's death, she surprised them all by taking a huge snorting breath which brought her back to life.

A fever raged through her body like a forest fire. Dalinda Scandone, who reluctantly took her turn at the watch, filled seven buckets by wringing out the sponge used to mop Ramona's brow. Dalinda's fear of contracting plague almost got the better of her, but her fear of Immacolata Metrofano was greater, and she mopped on with an unwilling heart, alternately uttering prayers and curses. As the buckets were passed along a human chain to be emptied, it was noted that the contents bore no odour. What a contrast to the days when the sweat would have been perfumed by the maddening aroma, and the men carrying the pails would have fought one another to the death for possession of a single drop.

Ramona did not make a sound. No moans, no sighs, no groans left her lips. No hallucinations teased her brain. In the sickroom and beyond, speculation was rife. What was the cause of this terrible ague that gripped her bones? Was it, as many claimed, the fever of divine retribution? Was Ramona at last paying the price of her wicked nature and indecent ways? What had happened to her in the big city? What had become of Rinaldo Buffi? What had led to her unwelcome reappearance here at La Casa? And what about the child? She was the biggest riddle of them all. She had been washed and fed properly for the first time in her life, and had fallen asleep making gurgling sounds that resembled singing. How could she have developed so quickly?

When the next day finally dawned, Ramona was still alive, but only just. The new doctor, Stipa, who now danced attendance on the ailing Signor, asked if he might take a look at the unusual patient. He wanted to see for himself the servant girl who had had such a devastating effect on his old med-school friend, Blocco. He was shocked. During their college days he had been aware that Blocco wore his heart on his sleeve. But this was ridiculous. This woman was a freak. How could such a creature have led him to take his own life? He would never understand it. Dr Stipa confidently predicted Ramona's imminent death, and left La Casa preparing to pay a visit on Blocco's widow on his way home. He had been at the wedding and seemed to remember that Alfonsina wasn't a bad looking girl.

Word of Ramona's return had travelled fast around the estate. The workers who did not live inside La Casa all hurried over and gathered in the yard unsure of what to do, but keen to be a part of the moment. Although it was widely broadcast that the smell had disappeared, none of them quite believed it until they entered the sickroom and took a deep sniff of the air circulating around the patient. Soon a queue was stretching from the yard through the kitchens and up the back stairs to the attic, of those who wanted to witness the phenomenon for themselves. Immacolata Metrofano objected to this intrusion into her kitchens, but decided it was best to allow nature to take its course. She hoped that once everyone had paid a visit, life would return to normal.

One of the first visitors was Trofimo Barile, the innkeeper, who took a professional interest in everything; it was his duty to keep his customers well informed. Predictably he was not in the least surprised by the strange turn of events and that evening was heard discoursing over the counter of the Black Toad on a similar case, involving a dairymaid who gave birth to a son already aged eleven.

Stiliano Mamiliano, the pig keeper, was a frequent visitor to the sickroom. At every opportunity his pigs afforded him, he would come sneaking in and surreptitiously stroke Ramona's hair. Sometimes he would whisper words into her ear, and although she was unconscious, he hoped she could hear him.

Stiliano's mother, Bibiana, and Ramona's other old adversaries, Saturnia Floscio, Gloriana Tomacelli and Andromeda Doria, lost no time in coming to gloat, and they sat around hoping that Ramona would take a turn for the worse. They had come prepared and

179

got out their knitting, the peas that needed shelling for supper and their backlog of darning, and looked for anything like the crones who gather at public executions. While they worked, they advised newcomers on Ramona Drottoveo's condition and waited optimistically for the worst to happen.

Milvia Lucentini, the midwife, was given charge of the child, who surprised everybody by telling them her name, 'Blandina'. Although she refused to answer any further questions, Blandina seemed to like singing, and even when she cried it was obvious she had perfect pitch. She had suffered no ill efects from the long journey and was soon running about in the Signora's garden, chasing the peacocks, plucking the orchids, and biting the under-gardeners with her sharp little teeth. Her hair was now so long it reached down to her middle, and as she ran it streamed behind her like a veil. Her features were finer than her mother's and she was a very pretty child, in spite of her unusual colouring. She would be a beauty in time, all who saw her agreed. As Milvia Lucentini ran after her, trying to prevent the girl from damaging the baby nectarines and trampling the violets, she couldn't help noticing Blandina was giving off a faint perfume. It was difficult to identify, but it was somehow familiar.

CHAPTER THIRTY-TWO

BEEF TEA

No-one liked to think of what might happen if Ramona recovered. At night the workers on the estate prayed for her speedy death. But above in the heavens, the Virgin Notburga, patron saint of servants, was toying with them all, alternately breathing life from her holy cheeks into Ramona Drottoveo's lungs, and then squeezing it out with her giant fingers.

Eventually, even those who hated Ramona most were growing bored with the upturns and downturns in her condition, which were broadcast regularly at the Black Toad. Then, at long last, the Virgin Notburga knew her entertaining game was over, and seemed to reach a decision.

'When I was yet a young man, in the region of Le Murge,' began Trofimo Barile one night, about a month after Ramona's return from Napoli, 'I met an old man who had been dying for forty years. One day he would get up from the sickbed and dance, the next he would be lying out stiff as a board, ready for burial. The day after that he would be playing a fiddle. Not that he was skilled in the manipulation of that instrument, but we can't all find favour with San Gregorio.

'Friends, one time we actually buried him, but then heard his raps on the coffin lid which forced us to dig him up again. He then performed the dance of the knives on his own grave. It went on and on. Those who were hale and hearty at the beginning of his long death went before him in legions to the grave. If his house hadn't caught fire after a lightning strike, he would still be with us now.

'Yes, friends, we must prepare ourselves: this situation could continue for years. We must not exhaust ourselves with expectation. The Good Lord will decide in his own due time.'

Amongst the listeners, Stiliano Mamiliano was the only one who did not accept the innkeeper's wisdom. Although he said nothing in the crowded bar, Stiliano had a strong feeling that Ramona's fate would soon be decided.

The following morning, early, he hurried through the gardens to La Casa, bounded up the back stairs and burst into the sickroom. In the very second that Stiliano entered, Ramona opened her eyes wide. Stiliano was the first person her glance rested upon, which he took to be a sign. Then, opening her lips, Ramona called out the word 'Breakfast.' Her voice was strong; there was no faltering. How strange it was that she knew the time of day, given that she had lain unconscious for a month.

Ramona Drottoveo was alive. There could

no longer be any doubt of that. Suddenly the room was full of people wanting to witness the awakening. Immacolata Metrofano pushed her way through the crowd—this was, after all, her territory.

'Dalinda Scandone,' she instructed, 'bring forth a cup of beef tea, and perhaps a little of the ewes' yoghurt mixed with honey. Something that doesn't tax the digestion.'

'Sausages,' cried Ramona, her pink eyes aflame. 'A suet pudding filled with tender chunks of beef in gravy. A whole buffalo mozzarella. Stewed apricots. A complete loin of pork. Snails. Ice-cream.'

All present held their breath and looked at Immacolata Metrofano who was bristling magnificently.

'Dalinda Scandone, bring forth the beef tea. Clearly, Ramona Drottoveo is delirious.' With that she swept from the room with the hauteur of the Signora, and went immediately to seek out her husband as he worked with his men repairing a hedge of hazels in the long boggy meadow.

'She's asking for sausages!' shrieked Immacolata with a red face while she was still some way off.

Semprebene clapped a hand to his face in despair. Now they were in for trouble.

Back in the sickroom, the hullabaloo died down and those who had pushed their way in to see Ramona Drottoveo come back to life pushed their way out again. Dalinda Scandone, as instructed, appeared with a small cup of beef tea, which she administered with a large spoon and little gentleness. Though disappointed at the failure of the sausages to appear, Ramona gulped down the broth like a drain.

'That's enough for you,' said Dalinda smugly as she snatched back the cup that Ramona was rinsing with her tongue. 'Immacolata Metrofano says you're to have nothing more until lunch, and then only a little yoghurt. The rest of us are having meatballs in tomato and mushroom sauce.'

Ramona made a rude gesture, but Dalinda had already turned her back. All the while Stiliano Mamiliano stood by the bedside awaiting his opportunity.

'Ramona Drottoveo,' he spoke out at last. 'It is I, Stiliano Mamiliano.'

Ramona looked at him squarely while casting around with her tongue for any drops of the broth that might have fallen on her cheeks and chin.

'I don't mind that the aroma has left you, Ramona. Anyways I think I prefer the odour of my pigs to any other smell in the world. I need no other scent. What I do need is a wife. I've asked all the other girls and they won't have me. It's the smell they object to, see, the smell of my pigs which clings to me like a damp vest. But I'll look after you, and the girl,

184

as if she were my own. My pigs approve the union. What do you say, Ramona Drottoveo, will you be my wife?' The words had all come out in a gush. Breathless, Stiliano Mamiliano waited for Ramona's response.

There was no trace of the broth anywhere on Ramona's face, and she had licked her lips until they were sore.

'I don't love you, it is true, Stiliano Mamiliano,' she said. 'And I recall from the one time I did it with you that your thing is very small. But will you feed me a roasted chicken with potatoes and rosemary? The egg-plant stuffed with tomato and *pecorino*? The lasagne, the *maccherone* baked with cheese, meat sauce, peas and egg? The cuttlefish stew? The pancake with . . .'

'Yes, yes, I'll feed you,' said Stiliano Mamiliano joyfully, caught up in the emotion of the moment. 'I keep a well-stocked larder. You'll want for nothing, Ramona Drottoveo, I promise you. And although you don't love me, I can accept that. All I ask is that you are kind to me, to me and my pigs.'

Before Ramona could answer, the bedroom door flew open, revealing a figure whose presence made Stiliano Mamiliano quiver and slink from the room without waiting to receive an answer to his proposal of marriage. The figure now filling the door frame was that of the Signor himself. He was livid that the news of his former favourite's return had been

185

withheld from him, and his face, badly scarred from the accident, was purple.

The Signor slammed the door behind him and throwing aside his riding crop he ran to the bed where he buried his head in Ramona's bosom, sobbing.

'Ahhhhh,' he gurgled, from memory inhaling deeply at the place he considered the fountainhead of the luscious aroma. 'Ahhhhh.'

It was some time before he could bring himself to surface. All the while he inhaled at her, Ramona looked down at him puzzled, awaiting the rejection which was sure to follow when he realized the scent had vanished. But miraculously the rebuff didn't come.

'At last, at last I have it in my nose again,' he sobbed, tears streaming down his frightful face. 'My darling, I can't fully express my joy at this moment.'

Here he broke down completely, and was unable to speak again for some time. Since the accident he had begun hearing voices inside his head, and when they spoke a glazed look would steal over his eyes while he listened to his instructions.

Ramona watched him intently, waiting for some clue as to what was going on. Finally the Signor nodded in agreement with the voices and answered, 'Yes, my leader,' before his eyes unfroze and he remembered what he had been saying.

'All through my terrible illness I have been

dreaming endlessly of your aroma. The quacks told me I would never recover my sense of smell, but you have proved them wrong. I have it now in my nose. Why, it is even more bewitching than it was before. Oh let me bury myself in it. Let me drown in it. Oh the ecstasy of it! Oh. Oh. Oh.'

So saying the Signor buried his head and indeed his whole person beneath the bedclothes, and when Immacolata Metrofano came in some time later to check on Ramona a look of horror set upon her face, showing that her worst fears had just been confirmed.

CHAPTER THIRTY-THREE

THE NEW SIGNORA

Despite the fact that La Casa was still in mourning, preparations for the wedding of the Signor and Ramona Drottoveo were soon steaming ahead. It was scandalous. Shocking. Throughout the region, right-minded people were outraged. After all, it was only three months since the accident. A mere twelve weeks from that terrible day when the gleaming automobile had been delivered; one of the first off the production line of the Fiat company in Torino.

Watched by the entire staff, who were

waving flags and cheering, the Signor was to drive the Signora on the inaugural run around the estate. The Signora was tucked in safely with travel rugs, furs, an umbrella, a smelling bottle, and a lucky charm dedicated to San Cristoforo, the patron saint of journeys.

Yet they had not left the confines of the stable yard before there was a noise like thunder and the engine exploded. The Signora was killed instantly, scattered to the four winds in a thousand fragments that could never be collected. The Signor was propelled through the air at a dangerous speed, and landed on his head on the dome of the *tempietto* to Apollo, with the steering wheel still in his hand. He escaped death, but his head suffered terribly.

The accident taught the Signor two important lessons: first, he would never again trust himself to a mode of transport that didn't involve a horse; and second, life was fragile, making him determined to seize the day. He would brook no opposition to his plans, and intended to marry Ramona Drottoveo without delay.

The Signor was besotted with the scent that he convinced himself he could smell despite the dreadful damage to his nasal passages. When the voices came they urged him to marry Ramona Drottoveo before someone could steal her and her aroma away from him. Although far from being fully recovered, he dismissed Dr Stipa and the other medical experts who he assumed were out to cheat him. Ramona Drottoveo was the only cure he needed. Her scent was an elixir, sufficient to restore a man to the peak of his condition. As master of the scent he would live for ever. And so the doctors packed up and left La Casa, shaking their heads and predicting the direst consequences.

Ramona Drottoveo made a rapid recovery from her illness and was already acting the part of the Signora, in whose rooms she had been installed. She wasted no time in having them refitted according to her gaudy taste. Blandina, in turn, was already acting the part of the Signorina, and was busy retouching the precious silk hangings of the ancestral nursery with crayons and paints.

When the servants learned of the impending alliance, many fell sick, and some even died. Stiliano Mamiliano quickly recovered from his disappointment, but was so afraid of being punished for making his proposal that he came out in hives. Dalinda Scandone began to have fits. Beata Viola developed a crepuscular rash. Ugo Rossi grew a third ear on the back of his head. Even those who didn't take to their beds experienced the whole gamut of emotions from disbelief to fury to despair, and were coloured by every delicate hue of misery in between. That Ramona Drottoveo of all people was to be their new mistress! It was like a bad joke. Except it wasn't at all amusing.

And with the smell gone, it was downright inexplicable.

If only the Signor could be made to see that his poor damaged brain was clinging to the memory of the scent rather than the scent itself. But who would be the one to tell him?

How could they, the women especially, wait upon Ramona Drottoveo? Oh, how their former mistress must be writhing in fury in her tomb. Immacolata Metrofano, the mother of the household, felt it keenest. Was this a judgment upon her for some past sin? She had one or two minor matters on her conscience, but these could not be responsible. Surely not. How could she be expected to bear it? This question framed itself in her mind a thousand times a moment. Yet there was never a satisfactory answer. Exhausted, she sank into a malaise as deep as the well shaft.

She no longer ruled the kitchens with a rod of iron. There was a rapid descent into chaos. The copper pots, no longer polished twice a day, grew smeary. Preserves and pickles went mouldy in the jars. Fish reeked. Maggots got their way with the meats. Wine was corked. Fruit and vegetables rotted. Rats got into the cellars where the dry goods were stored. Dirt gathered. Bacteria multiplied. Taking advantage of Immacolata Metrofano's distraction, Dalinda Scandone, whose cheeks had not felt a slap in weeks, indulged openly in immoral behaviour with Roberto Pedretti.

Immacolata Metrofano no longer seemed to take a pride in her cooking. She sent ducks to the table with their feathers still on and their entrails intact. Stale bread became a staple. Puddings lost their feathery lightness and became surly, weighty things that stuck like glue to the innards of those foolish enough to eat them. Pastry crusts on pies broke teeth on an unprecedented scale.

The sauces were full of lumps, and Ramona Drottoveo actually sent one back to the kitchens from the high table where she now took her meals. What ignominy! All the servants watched anxiously, not liking to imagine how the head cook would respond to such an insult. But even in the face of this shame Immacolata Metrofano didn't emerge from her depression.

Nobody could believe what had got into Immacolata Metrofano, and her new husband was terribly worried about her. After the Signor was served a live lobster which attacked his nose with its claws, Semprebene Metrofano knew he had to take a firm hand with his wife or they would be served their notice. After this, matters in the kitchen did improve, but Immacolata's spirit was crushed, and she never fully recovered.

Despair manifested itself all over the estate. In the gardens, fountains played the sound of weeping. The topiaries developed strange swellings. Cheeky greenfly infested the rose garden, causing Ernesto Conticello a heartache he had never previously known. Moles burrowed up, creating bumps on the perfect lawns. The buffaloes dried up and stopped giving milk, and nothing could be done to get them lactating again. In the dairy, cheeses curdled, butter went rancid. The lemon crop shrivelled. Turnips grew into bizarre shapes which indicated the presence of the devil. A swarm of angry hornets attacked a band of men working in the cherry orchard, with horrific consequences. Discontented labourers grew lazy and spent all their time complaining, and Semprebene Metrofano had to work day and night to hold things together. It reminded everybody of the terrible time of the beekeeper's death. What a scourge was Ramona Drottoveo. Would they never be free of her curse?

Some of the younger, more idealistic servants talked of resigning all at once, thereby showing the Signor what they thought of his choice. But having no other place to go, they would be the only ones to suffer from a mass walkout. There had to be another way. But nobody could think what it was.

The arrival of the Signor's married sister, the lady Margherita, from Potenza, inspired a glimmer of hope. She told her brother he was making a huge mistake, but the Signor wouldn't listen. Instead he blew up into a rage, and obeying the instructions of the voices, he threw her down the steps from the grand entrance. The cracked ribs and broken nose she sustained encouraged his other relatives to keep their lips firmly closed.

CHAPTER THIRTY-FOUR

THE WEDDING

The day of the wedding dawned with smoke-coloured clouds scudding across the sky. There was sure to be a storm, and the villagers scurried along to bag a space in the *chiesa* clutching their umbrellas. At the hour of the nuptials, the little church was straining at the seams with the weight of invited guests and gawping gatecrashers.

The pews were, of course, reserved for the persons of quality, and the common folk were obliged to squeeze in where they could. Trofimo Barile had managed somehow to get in between the Contessa Magina and the honourable Lady Lydia, the Signor's third cousin once removed. He was entertaining them with the story of the royal wedding he had once attended in the principality of Liechtenstein and the ladies were spellbound. The others, even such luminaries as Immacolata and Semprebene Metrofano, had to content themselves with standing at the back, and the likes of Stiliano Mamiliano and Virna Fuga, who were not pushy enough, got stuck behind the pillars.

The Signor stood at the high altar awaiting his bride, dressed in the uniform of the Hussars in which he had served the nation during the last war. The bullet holes had been expertly mended so that they hardly showed, and the right leg of the trousers that had been ripped off by the explosion was matched seamlessly so that even he was unsure of where the tear had been. The array of medals on his chest glittered brighter than the gold of the great cross on the altar.

The Signor paid no attention to the glorious gilt and marble tomb of his first wife which he passed on the way in. It towered above the nave, looking slightly incongruous in the surroundings which were uniformly faded, ramshackle and moth-eaten. His only thought was of Ramona, or more precisely, of the aroma, to which he would shortly be joined in matrimony.

While the guests waited, they were entertained by Blandina, who sang for them the *Panis Angelicus* and the Bridal Chorus from *Lohengrin*. She now resembled a child of seven, and was arrayed in a gown of white lace like a miniature bride. It was the Signor's idea. He was a passionate music lover, and was enchanted by his new stepdaughter's voice. Ramona was less delighted by Blandina's vocal gift, although she knew it did not rival her own. Nevertheless Ramona was irate that the child had inveigled her way into her special day. Still, she gritted her teeth and said nothing. She knew it would be unwise to start contradicting the Signor until after the ceremony.

At last Ramona Drottoveo arrived, fashionably late. As she stepped from the carriage she slipped on her train and almost fell onto the empty grave of her first husband, who, as a suicide, had been given the meanest spot in the churchyard. Perched on the decayed tombstones, on the porch and on the gargoyles were crows that gabbled in strange tongues at her approach. A streak of lightning cut open the sky that was now almost black. Vittorino Broschi, Ramona's one-time lover, the former postilion who had been elevated to the position of third assistant coachman, shivered. Ramona, however, was totally preoccupied with her own beauty and grandeur and was oblivious to these terrible portents.

When she made her grand entrance into the *chiesa*, the individual gulps of the congregation formed one massive gasp of disbelief. Ramona considered this a response to her incredible beauty, yet beauty was not how most people would have described it. The guests had never seen anything like it: the enormous crinoline, the immodest *décolletage*, the towering head-dress adorned with swans' feathers and tinkling bells, the bizarre goggles studded with rubies. The overall effect was monstrous. It was too much for the Signor's ancient aunt Crispina who collapsed in shock and died in the vestry before the conclusion of the service.

Ramona paraded down the aisle, which had been not only swept but polished in honour of the occasion, followed by a train a hundred metres long embellished with fifty thousand seed pearls sewn by seventy seamstresses who had worked around the clock in order to finish it in time.

Waiting for her, by the holy altar, was the Signor, who felt himself the luckiest man alive. As his friends sneered at his bride, the Signor mistook their disgust for the uncontrolled lust she used to arouse, and he felt an overpowering smugness that he had carried off the prize every other man in the world wanted.

Ramona was in heaven. At that defining moment all her dreams came true. She was indeed a fairy queen. No, not a fairy, a goddess. An empress, even. She was beautiful. She was about to be declared the Signora. All these fancy people were looking upon her with love and awe.

The Signor's friends were incredulous. He had been behaving strangely since the accident, but marrying this hideous and vulgar upstart confirmed that he had gone completely mad. His oldest friend the Duc'd'Alba considered calling a halt on the grounds of insanity, especially as the Signor continued to speak out to the voices in his head throughout the ceremony. But in the event *il duca* said nothing. Although many hoped the spectacle would yet turn out to be an elaborate hoax, it was not to be. The nuptials were conducted according to the holy law.

Later, at the wedding breakfast, there was enough food to feed five thousand guests. In her greed Ramona ordered this excess to be prepared, and although Immacolata Metrofano complained to the Signor, he told her to obey her new mistress and involve him no more in the running of the household.

In the servants' hall the feasting was half-hearted, for all were worried about what the future held.

'You'll be first to be whipped, Dalinda Scandone,' said Ugo Rossi, who now wore a cap indoors to hide his deformity. 'Ramona Drottoveo never could stand the sight of you.'

Dalinda Scandone slipped quietly into a fit as Beata Viola, swathed in crêpe bandages, toyed miserably with an artichoke.

'You'll be dismissed, Ugo,' she said. 'I've heard she's replacing all the under-butlers with young, handsome ones.'

'I'm young and handsome,' replied Ugo bravely, but he knew that with the third ear he didn't stand a chance.

In the salon, where the persons of quality

197

took light refreshments, Ramona alone retained her appetite, and did justice to the caviare canapés, the champagne sherbets, the truffle tartlettes, that Immacolata Metrofano and her team had spent all night preparing.

How Ramona loved to be waited upon by her former fellow servants! As they circulated amongst the guests, weighed down by the best silver salvers loaded with delicacies, she barked out her orders:

'You there, bring me more champagne. More of those little pastries. More cake.'

And the quaking footmen hurried to obey her. How wonderful it was to be the Signora.

The only minor irritant in an otherwise perfect day was Blandina. The guests petted her and made a fuss of her and kept asking her to sing. The girl revelled in their attention, and with sneering looks at her mother was not slow to put herself forward.

CHAPTER THIRTY-FIVE

THE WEDDING JOURNEY

The wedding journey to Paris was the flimsy stuff of Ramona's dreams made real. Every morning when she opened her eyes in their sumptuously appointed suite in the Hôtel de Crillon she was filled with joy that she hadn't awoken to her old life.

How wonderful was Paris! How much more beautiful than Napoli where she had once lived and which she had imagined the most sparkling place in the world. Why it was a mere village in comparison to Paris. Paris!

The newlyweds were deliriously happy. They shopped for gowns in the finest stores along the Rue du Faubourg St-Honoré; for shoes and hats in the arcades of the Palais Royal; for furs in the Avenue Montaigne; for jewels in the Rue de la Paix. Ramona's greedy eyes, framed now by a pair of fancy eyeglasses, fixed upon the finest fripperies and the Signor happily indulged her every whim. The sorority of chic sales ladies looked down upon the odd-looking whore and the horribly scarred old fellow who talked to himself, but when word circulated about the signor's wealth and position in his own country, they could not have been more charming.

Gowns were ordered, each style in every colour of the rainbow. The same for shoes and hats. The finest furs that could be trapped and subject to the furrier's arts were commissioned by the dozen. And jewels so magnificent they required the presence of an armed bodyguard, who walked alongside the page carrying the packages.

When they finished shopping, they would dine at Le Grand Véfour, at Bofinger, or Les Ambassadeurs, where Ramona's unusual table manners, the loud slurping noises, and the gnawing of bones, mesmerized the other diners with a revulsion which was compelling. They would take a stroll along the *grands boulevards* or a carriage ride out to the Bois de Boulogne. In the evening they frequented the cabaret at the *Folies Bergère* or visited the Opéra Garnier.

The opera! How Ramona loved the opera. Had her life turned out differently it could have been her down there on the stage. What a Mimi she would make! What a Carmen! Why, the roles could have been written for her. Bewigged, powdered, rouged, and dressed in a way that would have outshone Marie-Antoinette, Ramona sat in her box hypnotized by the performance, oblivious to the fact that the rest of the audience had forgotten the production and the lorgnettes of the entire opera house were turned towards her in utter disbelief.

The Signor, however, was not oblivious to this. Far from it. The general astonishment he took for admiration, and congratulated himself wholeheartedly on securing the new Signora over every other man. She, who could have had anybody! She had preferred him, even to those who were firm in body as well as mind and were not afflicted with his many disorders. During this phase in his life, the voices in his head were at their most benevolent, and they too congratulated him on his choice. The terrible tic that sometimes seized hold of his scarred face and would not let go was dormant throughout the honeymoon, and after their frenzied lovemaking he slept the sleep of the dead: his insomnia had vanished. He felt good for the first time since the accident. And he never tired of thanking the scent for it. He loved more than anything to bury his head in Ramona's bosom and take great gasping gulps of the phantom fragrance. He could feel it restoring him, and Ramona, who was happier than she had ever been, was delighted to indulge him.

The only fly in Ramona's ointment was that she no longer had her aroma. If she had it now, the whole of the glittering city of Paris would be at her feet. The princes and the emperors and all the handsome foppish Frenchmen would be fighting duels over her. If only she hadn't had the child, she would have it still. Blandina had of course been left on the estate in the care of Milvia Lucentini. Another of the many benefits of being the Signora was that she didn't have to bother about the girl any more. In fact she had almost succeeded in forgetting all about her.

Yet all too soon Ramona was calling upon the Holy Virgin to bless her new union with offspring. One evening as they strolled along the Seine, the Signor, in a rare moment of lucidity, explained what would happen if he remained childless. An entailment gave him the estate for his lifetime only, and on his death without issue, it would pass back into the hands of his first wife's family, to whom it rightfully belonged and who had owned it for generations.

At this news Ramona was ready to collapse. Her new and wonderful life was in jeopardy! Why, the Signor was old. He was as rickety in body as in mind. He could be carried off at any moment. Every morning she half expected to find his corpse curled up beside her in the bed. Then the fairytale life she had worked so hard for would be snatched away, and she would be ruthlessly cast out. She knew the old Signora's brother at Roccamonfina would lose no time in stripping her of her finery and shutting his doors in her face. She saw in her mind's eye the servants' jubilation at her ignominious expulsion from the estate. There was no time to lose.

Immediately she rushed the Signor back to the suite. There she ripped off his clothes and hurried to enervate his flaccid penis. She had to conceive. Each day without a child was a day lived in danger. The Signor was delighted by the newfound ardour of his bride, and with the help of medication and a small rubber pump he was able to acquit himself creditably for a man his age. His happiness increased. She loved him. There was no doubt of that. He was the luckiest man alive.

For the remainder of the wedding journey

Ramona forsook the shops and confined the Signor to the suite, where she employed all her arts and made completely unreasonable demands upon him. They were the happiest days of his life. But when the time came to return home, there was no baby; it was the only cloud in an otherwise dazzling sky.

CHAPTER THIRTY-SIX

THE HOMECOMING

Ramona returned to the estate with fifty trunks of gowns, twenty-seven of shoes, eleven of hats, five of furs, and an oversize strongbox containing the finest jewels Paris had to offer. All hands were required to assist with the carrying in, and in doing so Ugo Rossi sustained a hernia which added to the general rancour.

Blandina danced down the steps as soon as the carriage came into view. She had grown much taller since the wedding, and was graceful and slender and lovely. She could now pass for a child of ten or twelve. Blandina ignored her mother completely, but threw herself into the arms of the Signor, who kissed her fondly. He had bought her some special gifts in Paris and was anxious to give them to her.

The porters were amazed at the way the Signor bounded up the steps holding his stepdaughter's hand. In the past he had had to be carried. The months away had a restorative effect on him, and he was looking ten years younger than he had before the marriage. Ramona Drottoveo really was good for him: even the most bitter of the servants had to admit that.

The new Signora, indignant at her daughter, oversaw the unpacking with much fussiness and fault-finding. She then conducted an inspection of the grounds that were now hers, and which had gradually recovered from the disorder they had fallen into following her reappearance at La Casa. How far had she come from the days when she was banned from the gardens by the old Signora, and although she had persisted in getting in, she had had to be furtive about it.

Now, resplendent in a gown of Versailles lace, she paraded around beneath a matching parasol held up for her by Ovidio Gondulfo, the head gardener, who had once been so in love with her that he licked the place where her feet had walked. There was no trace of that emotion now however, and the head gardener bristled like one of his prize cacti at being made to carry her umbrella.

Ramona revisited all her old haunts. She strolled along the manicured parterres where the perfect grass perfumed the air with the

204

smell of mint and was as springy as a trampoline.

The rose garden was back in finest form, and not a single greenfly could be found among the three thousand varieties tended with such love by Ernesto Conticello and his team. Ovidio Gondulfo bristled more at the ignominy of being seen by his subordinates holding a sunshade over Ramona Drottoveo, and he noted with a narrow eye those unwise enough to allow a smirk to contort their faces.

The scent in the rose garden had such intensity that it carried for miles upon the breeze, but all had to admit it was a pale shadow of the aroma Ramona Drottoveo herself once had. The air was alive with the buzzing of bees, and brightly coloured butterflies fluttered, forming a constantly changing kaleidoscope. The box hedges and dolphin topiaries were clipped to perfection. Fountains played. Stone lions roared, scaring chubby *putti*. The lily beds were just as magnificent as Ramona remembered them: the flawless flutes of creamy white set amidst furling curls of deep green leaves. She would have a great many picked and sent to her rooms.

In the walled vegetable gardens, Ramona wandered between the neat rows where everything from asparagus to zucchini was sprouting in the rich soil. Beyond, in the pig yard, Stiliano Mamiliano was preparing a foul-smelling swill. He doffed his cap and actually bowed as she approached. She had to laugh: as if she would have agreed to marry the pig keeper! Why, she was half inclined to have him whipped for his impudence. Instead she decided to order a great deal of pork at luncheon; she knew what slaughtering his pigs cost poor Stiliano.

Curiosity then drove her to take a look at the beekeeper's cottage: the humble cottage where she had twice been taken as a bride. To think she once lived in a place that size! Now her wardrobes were bigger by far than this cottage. If only the Signora had died sooner, Ramona would have been saved so much suffering. Still, she wasn't bitter, and she smiled sweetly as Ovidio Gondulfo introduced her to the new beekeeper, Nuccio Pandolfo.

Earnestly he showed her his innovations: the increased number of hives to which the busy buzzing bees were returning from the rose garden laden with pollen and self-importance. He showed her a new queen, of a disease-resistant strain he was hoping to introduce. Ramona indulged him by feigning interest. What did she care about bees? She was the queen bee herself.

Although he was a fine, upright young man, with blond hair and sturdy thighs, she wasn't even tempted. She was far too fine a lady now to be interested in a rough working man. And she would on no account be unfaithful to the

Signor. Never would she give her enemies the opportunity of saying the child she was determined to conceive wasn't her husband's.

Having conducted her tour, she had Ovidio Gondulfo lead her back to the conservatory, where she ordered a jug of lemonade and drained it noisily. She was highly satisfied with everything, but thought it fitting to order alterations. She was the Signora now after all, and it was right the servants should do her bidding. So she set about explaining to the head gardener what changes she expected him to make in the life of the garden. Yes, the gardens that had remained unchanged for hundreds of years were to be replanted according to Ramona's taste. Ovidio Gondulfo blanched like an almond, and tried to protest, but Ramona would not listen. When he was finally dismissed, the head gardener took himself to the compost heap where he threw himself down and wept.

Next Ramona summoned Immacolata Metrofano to discuss the changes she wished to see in the running of the household. During the months of the honeymoon the head cook had recovered from her depression, and something of the old fire flared in her eyes as she listened to Ramona's instructions. When she returned to the kitchens, the cheeks of Dalinda Scandone were quick to feel a shower of slaps, which they had grown unused to of late.

207

CHAPTER THIRTY-SEVEN

THE PERFORMANCE

One morning, not long after the newlyweds' return, La Casa awoke to the sound of hammering and sawing. Ramona was having an opera house built in the grounds, on the far side of the grotto of the nymphs, and three hundred labourers had been brought in to hurry the construction to a quick completion. There, Ramona would give her own performances.

She had formed her own operatic company, of which she, naturally, was the star. She engaged a singing teacher and worked tirelessly at her lessons, although the Signor was the only one able to detect an improvement in her limited ability. While Ramona struggled over her scales, Blandina could be heard around La Casa singing pure, clear notes, and the music master wept at being denied access to such a rare talent.

The Signor continued to thrive, in body but not in mind. His obsession with the scent took some bizarre turns. Ramona had grown accustomed to him following her around like a dog, sniffing at her. And when he couldn't sit with his head buried in her lap, he insisted on carrying an item of her clothing around with him, like a child with a comfort blanket. He had started talking to the aroma, having identified it with a particularly soft female voice inside his head. He wrote poetry to the scent and recited it. He had taken up painting and started painting pictures of it.

Ramona indulged his funny little ways, but his obsession did cause her the occasional flicker of anxiety. Once she had a nightmare in which he recovered the ability to smell. He realized that she no longer exuded the fleshy-bodied aroma that formed the touchstone of his life. She awoke in a sweat, and although it was yet the middle of the night, she rang for Belinda Filippucci, her personal maid, to change her nightgown and bed linen.

Yet Ramona was not often plagued by nightmares. Usually she slept the sleep of the dead, and snored, some said, loud enough to raise them too. She had to admit the notion of the Signor recovering his sense of smell was unlikely, yet the Signor's senses were a law unto themselves. Each day there was some change. Some days he would be profoundly deaf. Some days too he would lose his sense of balance, and keep toppling over. Then he would recover his hearing and lose all sensation of taste. At such times he could not distinguish between the taste of a pear and a partridge, a boar sausage and a butterscotch pudding, and no efforts of Immacolata Metrofano could please him. The one constant was his belief in that wonderfu aroma in his nose, and it gave him comfort in a scary world.

There was still no sign of the baby they both longed for, but they never gave up hope, and their attempts to spawn one, given the Signor's infirmities, took up much time. Ramona was resentful of Blandina, her first-born, who was growing bigger and more bothersome by the day. How unfair it was that the unwanted child thrived while the desired one had not been given life. If only she could send Blandina back and replace her with the Signor's child. So much depended upon a new baby.

Ramona started to think Blandina had put the evil eye upon her and that this was the reason the new baby didn't come. Right from the start she had not liked the looks the child had given her. The girl clearly hated her. In the early days Ramona had pretended a certain fondness for the child in front of the Signor, but she had long since given that up.

Although her mother shunned her, the Signor was enormously fond of Blandina. She was the daughter he had never had, and she reminded him of how Ramona would have been as a girl. They shared interests in music and horses. She sang for him his favourite arias. When he was able, they rode out together around the estate. He spoiled her and petted her. She had everything and more than a girl could dream of, and this further annoyed Ramona, for she felt the difference from her own childhood in the convent under the harsh regime of the nuns. She was jealous in retrospect. Her resentment of the child increased, and the child hated her mother even more.

Yet it would be wrong to think Ramona wasted too many of her thoughts on her daughter. No. The opening night at the opera house was fast approaching, and she had so much to do to get everything ready. As well as bullying the upholsterers who were slow to finish, Ramona had endless costume fittings, and she had to instruct Stiliano Mamiliano in his part. On account of his beautiful baritone he was selected to accompany Ramona in duets, and although he was most reluctant to appear, he knew he had no choice. Ramona was aware that his presence reduced the class of the act, yet she needed his voice. But as he wasn't to be illuminated—for all the spotlights were to be trained on Ramona—she hoped he would be heard but not seen.

Magnificent invitations on thick card with gold writing were sent out to all the Signor's former friends, but not a single one accepted, for they had closed ranks against the vulgar Signora. Ramona cried bitter tears at this, the first she had shed since her marriage, and the Signor was furious. Determined not to disappoint his wife, he issued an edict that all the servants and workers on the estate were to attend. Although many would have liked to boycott the event, they were not too proud to accept free entertainment, and curiosity about the opera house got the better of them.

The interior was magnificent. Trofimo Barile, the only member of the audience who had been inside a proper opera house, declared himself satisfied that every detail was correct. The rich red carpets, the endless mirrors, the gilt, the chandeliers, the velvet drapes and seats: he examined them all closely and could only praise their quality, although the opera house of his brother-in-law's neighbour's cousin's employer was somewhat more opulent. The less sophisticated folk were awestruck. It truly was a palace.

Ramona was taking no chances, and the audience was issued with clear instructions about when to clap loudly, when to give a standing ovation, and when to throw the flowers they had been supplied with for the purpose. She would have preferred persons of her own rank and standing to witness her glittering début, but a part of her gloried in the fact that her former colleagues would be there.

Trofimo Barile had scarcely embarked on a story he heard as a young barman working at La Fenice in the beautiful city of Venezia when the hundred-piece orchestra struck up the overture from the great pit beneath the stage, and the wise man was silenced. The acoustics were perfect, everybody had to agree.

There was a delicious feeling of expectation as the waited for Ramona Drottoveo to appear. Indeed Dalinda Scandone, who had not known such excitement since the fête when Ramona went away, fainted and had to be carried outside. She saw nothing of the performance.

The crowd, sitting in silence, held their breath and waited. Backstage, Ramona felt the agreeable sensation of butterflies in her stomach. It was exactly as the precious dream she had in Napoli while waiting for Signor Po to call her to the San Carlo. All this time she had nurtured that dream. Now she had recreated it, and made it real. If only Signor Po could see her now.

Finally it was time, more than time, and the Signor, sitting on a stool in the wings and clutching one of her stockings to his nose, blew her a kiss just as the curtains opened. There was a gasp from the staff that rose above the sound of the orchestra, who were then giving it their all. Ramona Drottoveo was scarcely recognizable. No expense had been spared in the creation of the wig and the costume which glittered brighter than the chandeliers from all the *diamanté* embroidery on it.

She stepped forward, and gave a low, deep curtsy. The vision may not have resembled the old Ramona Drottoveo, but the sound that emerged from between her painted lips certainly did. It was Ramona Drottoveo all right, and many wished they had brought along tufts of wool to stuff into their ears. Ugo Rossi was in agony.

Ramona's rendition of *O mio babbino caro* would doubtless have caused irreparable hearing damage to many, had not Semprebene Metrofano, ever vigilant, noticed that the auditorium had become filled with a choking black smoke, whereupon the performance was cruelly interrupted by the members of the audience abandoning their seats and running for their lives.

Fortunately no lives were lost, although Stiliano Mamiliano suffered terrible burns to his legs, and all his hair fell out in shock. The sumptuous opera house was destroyed completely in four minutes, some two hours before the estate's antiquated fire wagon could be marshalled and rolled to the spot.

As Ramona sobbed at the curtailment of her début and the devastation of her opera house, Blandina was seen escaping from the burning building with a box of matches and a can of paraffin in her hands. As she ran away, singing like an angel, there was a smell in the air that was quite distinct from the acrid fumes of burning. It was a smell that struck a chord with many of the fleeing villagers, but they did not have occasion to remark upon it until much later.

CHAPTER THIRTY-EIGHT

A CROP OF BOYS

As Ramona surveyed the glowing embers of her dream, she accepted the sign, and vowed never to sing again. Eardrums all over the estate were saved.

Her fury burned brighter than the blaze when she discovered that Blandina was responsible for starting the inferno that had made her a laughing stock. She chased the girl round and round La Casa brandishing the Signor's riding crop, but Blandina was too fast for her. As she ran, Blandina sang tauntingly an off-key and all together diabolical rendition of *O mio babbino caro* in a voice uncannily like her mother's. Ramona was incandescent with rage.

Defeated, Ramona stamped off to find her husband and voiced her intention of sending Blandina to a convent to be raised, but the Signor wouldn't agree. He adored his stepdaughter and wouldn't hear of sending her away. How Ramona boiled when she found the Signor was not as compliant about the child as he was with all her other whims. As a result she withheld the smell from him for two days as a punishment, and although it was torture for him, he still wouldn't give in to her demands. It was their first disagreement about the child, but it wasn't the last.

That same day luncheon was late, which increased Ramona's ire, and it was exacerbated further when the reason for the delay was uncovered: Immacolata Metrofano had given birth to a son. It was surprising not just because Immacolata Metrofano was not in the first flush of youth, but also because, paying heed to superstition and local folklore, she had told no-one she was pregnant.

Blandina was not slow to parade little Sebaldo before her stepfather.

'Look at the pretty baby, Papa,' she said. 'I wish I could have such a sweet baby brother. But Mama doesn't make one.'

The poor Signor, who was having a confused day, initially thought the baby he had been shown was his own, and with joy coursing through his arrhythmic heart he hurried to find his sulking wife to congratulate her. Ramona had to disillusion the Signor, and was herself deeply wounded. She hadn't expected such treachery from Immacolata Metrofano. She let it be known that she didn't wish there to be any further births amongst the servants in advance of her own.

Blandina quickly abandoned the baby, with which she had grown bored, and ran to join her companions in the apple orchard. The girls on the estate avoided her, but the boys were drawn to her, and although she looked down

216

upon them, being the Signorina, she enjoyed teasing them. She made them do mischief to win her favour, and she liked nothing more than to get them into trouble.

Once she had Maurilio Bergonzoni, son of the cowman, steal the honeycombs from Nuccio Pandolfo's hives, and Maurilio suffered such an allergic reaction to the bee stings he sustained that for a while his life hung in the balance, and those who remembered the first beekeeper's death thought history was repeating itself. Blandina laughed at Maurilio's injuries and everybody had to admit she was her mother's daughter.

Andromeda Doria's wooden leg soon suffered a mishap at Blandina's instigation. So too did Bibiana Mamiliano's teeth; Stiliano Mamiliano's piglets; Ernesto Conticello's roses; Immacolata Metrofano's roast woodcocks; Ramona's wardrobes; and even the Signor's ear trumpet and other medical equipment. Nobody was safe from her japes.

Yet the local boys could only supply so much amusement. They were, after all, far too ignorant and boorish to make satisfying companions for such a sophisticated girl.

Following the fire, the Signor installed a governess at La Casa, despite the protests of his wife. His stepdaughter was a gifted student. Blessed with a natural intelligence, Blandina was soon fluent in four languages. She excelled at algebra and geometry. She knew the laws of

217

astronomy, biology, chemistry and physics. She was well versed in world history, geography and religion. She could argue politics. She loved literature. She wrote poetry. She could dance classical as well as folk dances. She could play the flute, the harp and the piano. But her greatest gift of all was her voice.

Blandina's voice was the sorest spot on the veritable rash of Ramona's resentments against her daughter. Her beautiful voice echoed around La Casa, filling it perpetually with song, and filling her mother's heart with rancour. Ramona no longer felt she had the upper hand and she didn't like it. She cursed herself when she remembered how she had returned for the child after abandoning her on the way back to the estate. If she had known then what a viper she had nourished in her womb she would never have retraced her steps.

Blandina, for her part, clearly remembered being left in the ditch by her mother, abandoned to passing wolves and vagabonds, and she was determined to get revenge in every way possible.

Ramona began to dwell on her own misfortune in producing such a child. What an unlucky woman she was. She fantasized about getting rid of Blandina. Why had she not given her to gypsies when she had the chance? Sold her into slavery? Left her as a foundling in the care of the Church, as she herself had been?

What had been good enough for her was good enough for the child. She could only blame herself for not acting at the time, but how could she have predicted the way things would turn out?

Following the birth of Sebaldo Metrofano, Milvia Lucentini died of an embolism that had caused her body to swell up like a whale. It was Milvia who had schooled Blandina in the use of the potty, trained her lisping speech and pulled out her loosened milk teeth. It was Milvia who tended Blandina through every childhood illness: the measles, the chickenpox, the mumps and the meningitis. She had dressed her grazed knees, eased her earache with the castor oil, and brushed the knots out of her hair. Milvia watched her with pride as she blossomed into an accomplished young woman. Yet at her death Blandina did not shed a single tear, and was unable to attend the funeral because she had an urgent engagement with her pony. The mourners saw her in the distance, jumping hedges and ditches with squeals of delight, dressed in the magnificent riding habit that had just arrived from Weatherill of London.

When the grass had grown over the grave of Milvia Lucentini, the marriage of Dalinda Scandone and Robert Pedretti took place at the Chiesa di San Stefano, and despite Ramona's strictures there followed many births, necessitating a great many baptisms.

Trofimo and Isolda Barile were surprised in their fifth decade by an heir to their thriving business empire. Immacolata Metrofano, encouraged by one success, subsequently brought forth twins, Casto and Polo. After that, Camilla Conticello, Margherita Rossi, Virna Fuga, Beata Viola, Andromeda Doria, Selma Venerosa and even Bibiana Mamiliano all produced sons. So many baby boys were born on the estate that people began to suspect there was something in the water.

Ramona alone remained without the son she so desperately wanted.

CHAPTER THIRTY-NINE

BLANDINA BLOSSOMS

Ramona experimented with every remedy and old wives' tale to try and aid conception. She tried regimens of figs, the well-known cure for infertility in the region, but although she experienced some effects as a result, pregnancy wasn't one of them. She fed the Signor on the testicles of rams and bulls, but apart from a noticeable increase in facial hair, and in the length of his ears, there was no obvious sign that his virility had been enhanced.

She tried over the months a multitude of

medical prescriptions: balms, embrocations, pills, syrups, suppositories and inhalants. After science failed her she tried rituals involving eggs. She made a pilgrimage to the standing stone at Formicola. She made votive offerings to Santa Margherita, patron saint of childbirth. She threw baby shoes into the sacred well at San Leucio. Yet she was not blessed, and she had to watch the crop of servants' sons growing up on the estate as strong and sturdy as ears of wheat.

While everybody else with the exception of the Signor considered Ramona's infertility a judgment upon her for her wicked ways, with her usual stubbornness she would not accept the inevitable. Nevertheless, as though hedging her bets, at this time she embarked upon a programme designed to prolong the life of the Signor. She made the doctors who had failed her in the field of fertility prescribe special diets for him, and he was deprived of coffee, alcohol, tobacco, red meat, cheese, eggs, salt, celery, apples, chocolate, and virtually everything else he enjoyed. Instead they gave him pills, medicines, suppositories and enemas.

Ramona had Nuccio Pandolfo produce extra supplies of royal jelly which she fed the Signor from a spoon into his toothless gums; for she knew the previous Signora had sworn by it as a means of prolonging life and vigour. She kept her husband a virtual prisoner in the bedroom, and would have wrapped him up in cotton wool if she could, but she hadn't reckoned with the Signor's own caprices.

He put up with a lot before the voices in his head set up a protest at the healthy lifestyle, and he rebelled. As well as smoking and drinking more than he had ever done in his life, the Signor spent more time in the saddle, a pursuit which caused Ramona more anxiety than all his other vices combined.

One morning the Signor came back from a ride with his stepdaughter who was now a fine young woman who looked seventeen, or thereabouts, and reported to his wife that the horses had been acting strangely. They were skittish and jumpy, and several of the hunters out at grass had broken from the field and galloped in a herd behind Blandina, neighing loudly in a way the Signor had never known. He called for the veterinary surgeon to be brought in, for he reasoned the horses had succumbed to colic or to some kind of foot rot, but this news struck terror into Ramona's heart.

The truth was that at puberty the smell which had been lying dormant within Blandina, emerging only occasionally and in a harmless way, now burst forth in all its fleshy glory. Ramona, who had never been able to smell the scent when she herself had it, could not detect it in her daughter, and because of the blockage in his nasal passages, neither could the Signor. Yet soon the insidious and intoxicating smell was penetrating every nook and cranny on the estate.

In recent weeks dogs had begun to follow Blandina around. In time they were joined by cats, squirrels, mules, chickens, buffaloes, mice, geese and, as reported by the Signor, horses. When she happened to pass the pig yard to torment Stiliano Mamiliano, the pigs with their sensitive noses set up such a squealing that the pig keeper had difficulty in calming them.

All too soon, the scent, plump, pulsating and positively indecent, was hanging heavy in the air and every man and boy with a working nose was its willing slave. It was just as sumptuous as it had been in Ramona's day, maybe even more so, and wives, mothers, mistresses and sweethearts cursed the history that was repeating itself.

Blandina herself, feeling the rampaging hormones of a teenager, was not long blind to her power. Soon she found two or three young men amongst the cloddish bumpkins whom she did not find positively repulsive.

Ramona knew all too well what had caused the stampede of horses, and it wasn't a case of the colic or the foot rot. She seethed with jealousy at the realization that Blandina would now have the world at her feet, as Ramona had had it in the past. She had stolen Ramona's scent! Yes, stolen it.

223

After the Signor left the room, Ramona flung herself onto the bed and sobbed. She pounded at the pillows with her fists as though pummelling her child. What an unnatural, ungrateful, evil girl she was, and with all the sacrifices Ramona made in her name! Always putting the child first, and herself last! She had lavished care, time and attention on her, had given her every possible advantage in life. She howled in fury at the injustice of it all.

She knew Blandina's evil ways. She would be sure to exploit the smell by every means possible. If she could, she would use it against her mother. Ramona prayed long and fervently that the Signor would never recover his sense of smell. If he did, she was frightened for her own future.

When she finished praying she was seized suddenly with determination. She would destroy the smell before it could destroy her. That was what she had to do. There had to be a way of stopping it, in this age of medical pioneering. And Ramona would find that way.

CHAPTER FORTY

REMEDIES

Without delay Ramona rang the bell for Dr Stipa, who was retained to treat Ramona for infertility and the Signor for infertility, longevity and, if possible, rejuvenation. She explained the situation to him, and although he produced a vial of green powders and some red pills from his medical bag, he couldn't dredge up any enthusiasm for the project. He had fallen helplessly, hopelessly, endlessly in love with Blandina. He was prepared to die for her, and that evening he would tell Alfonsina he was seeking an annulment of the marriage. Life had, since the day before, lost all meaning for him. If he didn't have Blandina soon, he would burst.

Ramona administered the drugs by slipping them into Blandina's food and wine at dinner, and then waited anxiously for the result. But at breakfast the following morning, although the girl complained that her sleep had been interrupted by flatulence and that her urine had turned purple, the actions of the footmen serving the coffee and rolls were a sure sign that Stipa's medications had not in any way diminished the potency of the scent. Ramona hoped her husband would not notice the shame of his serving men, and she herself developed a dose of indigestion which impaired her usually hearty appetite. Yet she need not have worried about the Signor. The voices were debating with him the relative merits of two new racehorses he was considering buying, and he was totally immersed in his own world. In addition his cataracts were particularly viscous today, although yesterday he had seen well enough to beat Blandina at archery.

After breakfast was over, Ramona summoned Stipa and told him he had to do better. His track record was not impressive and if he failed her again he would be relieved of his duties. He thus found himself in a difficult position: leaving the place where Blandina was would cause him to die immediately of a broken heart, but the condition of his staying was that he destroy the smell that was dearer to him than his own life. Despite his passion, he was a pragmatist, and he produced purgatives and potions, embrocations and emollients, lubricants and liniments which he was relieved to discover had no effect whatsoever.

That night as the doctor, who had left his wife, brooded in a booth at the Black Toad where he had taken up residence as an emergency measure, Trofimo Barile, understanding the cause of his sour expression, treated him to one of his stories.

'When I was at market in Sparanise the other week, I called in on my brother-in-law Silvestro, who keeps the Dancing Bear there. As I ate a veal pie for my lunch, a fine pie, light as air, Silvestro entertained me with the most extraordinary tale. A tale which may prove a solace to you in your predicament, Doctor. The case concerns a young man who goes by the name of Perseo, who, believe it or not, smelled strongly of onions. Yes, onions. Yes, friends, gather round, there's room for you all,' said Trofimo, breaking off to allow those drinkers who loved a good story to get into the booth with them.

'He was beginning to despair of ever taking a bride, for every girl in the region fled upon catching a whiff of him, when a wise old woman came to the door of his house. Wrapped in a cloak that obscured her face from view she said to him: "Perseo, you must feed on cheese, nothing but cheese: curds, gorgonzola and mozzarella. Thus you will rid yourself of the smell of onions and find a bride to fill your lonely bed."

'So saying, the old woman disappeared, before the young man could put so much as a single question to her. Was he to remain on a diet of cheese for the rest of his life? Could the cheese be cooked, or was it to be taken raw? Still, she had gone, and so he could not ask.

'Perseo was full of doubts, but he was so desperate he was prepared to try anything. He

227

decided to stock his larder with cheeses, and give the old woman's remedy a trial.

'For supper that night he tucked into a great slab of gorgonzola, for breakfast a plate of fluffy curds, and for lunch a whole buffalo mozzarella. And so it went on. Cheese. More cheese. Cheese took over his life. He dreamed of cheese. Finally he felt as though he was going mad, and always was the taste of cheese in his mouth.

'Yet, after a few days, the stench of onions was on the wane and after a week on this regimen the overpowering stink was gone. Before the wax and wane of the next moon he was married to a cheese-maker's daughter, with a little one already on the way. And so there you have it, learned Doctor, friends. A true story told to me only last week by my brother-in-law Silvestro Barbalace at the Dancing Bear in Sparanise.'

Being a medical man, Dr Stipa was sceptical to say the least, but he mentioned the matter in passing to his employer the next day.

'Trofimo Barile is a wise man,' said Ramona, after listening to the tale with all her ears. 'Immacolata Metrofano!' she then bellowed. 'Have Selma Venerosa bring up a basket of the buffalo mozzarella, and bring it now.'

Despite Blandina's allergy to cheese, Ramona locked herself into her daughter's chamber with the mozzarella at the ready, but at the end of a vicious afternoon during which both received an equal share of bites, black eyes, scratches, pinches and hair pulls, not a morsel of the mozzarella had passed Blandina's lips.

Dr Stipa listened to the rumpus from outside the room, and had the key not been turned on the inside, he would have entered the chamber and strangled his employer for her cruel assault upon his darling.

When Ramona emerged bruised and bleeding from the room, she gave Stipa a blistering look and hastened to find Semprebene Metrofano to discover when Trofimo Barile's lease on the Black Toad was up for renewal. The innkeeper was a fool. She had long been convinced of it.

After the failure of the cheese cure, Ramona tried more underhand means to eradicate the aroma. She acquired astringent soaps from a pharmaceutical chemist in Cancello Arnone, but the ulcers caused to her own flesh when she attempted to bathe her daughter with them forced her to abandon the scheme. She ordered in spells from a witch in Telese, but although she brewed up foul potions containing tongue of toad, wing of bat and ear of mouse, nothing worked.

The aroma was ever more resplendent and it carried on the breeze over immense distances, reaching even the noses of the Signor's former friends who lived on estates in the far reaches of the province. These gentlemen could not but obey the siren call of the scent, and many rode over to renew their friendship with the Signor and feast their noses on the luscious aroma of his delicious stepdaughter.

The Signor, who had long since forgotten that they had shunned his house since his marriage, welcomed them as though he had last seen them only yesterday. The gentlemen were amazed to find him in such apparently robust health. His appalling wife had been good for him, they had to admit. What a sly old fox he was! For a stepdaughter like that any one of them would have fought a duel for the privilege of marrying the mother.

These *signori* competed with one another for Blandina's notice and she treated them all with the utmost ruthlessness, which increased their ardour like nothing else.

Ramona, who had been taken over by her determination to destroy the scent, had neglected to enforce the Signor's strict regime. Taking advantage of his wife's preoccupation, he slipped out of La Casa. Lifted by the stable boys onto his prize hunter, Tullio, he joined his friends for a gallop over the fields in pursuit of a fox.

Scenting Blandina, who was at the front of the throng, the fox stopped running away and started running towards her, for its nose was confused by the succulent aroma suffusing the air. As a result the bloodhounds were thrown into disarray, and they got under the hoofs of the horses. The horses bucked and reared and bolted, and while two of the gentlemen were killed outright, the Signor was more fortunate. Tullio performed a somersault while straddling a hedge, and the Signor was propelled through the air in slow motion, during which time he enjoyed a heated debate with his voices on the subject of blends of tobacco. Thus he vaulted two fields of young barley, and came to rest finally on his head in a patch of clover amongst a herd of goats.

CHAPTER FORTY-ONE

IN WHICH THE SIGNOR
CLINGS TO LIFE

Once again, the Signor was on the brink of death. All the staff of La Casa experienced *déjà vu*. It was exactly as it had been after his first accident, except now Ramona Drottoveo was a constant presence at his bedside, mopping his brow with a sea sponge, spooning medicine between his dry lips, and haranguing the doctors who had not suceeded in accelerating his recovery.

Immacolata Metrofano, who now brought all Ramona's meals to the dimly lit sickroom, remarked to her husband that night, after she had put her three boisterous boys to bed, that Ramona Drottoveo did seem genuinely fond of the Signor, for she tended him with infinite care and worried looks through every hour of the day and night.

Did Ramona Drottoveo have a heart after all? Was she capable of love? Or was it that the awful consequences of the Signor's death were at the front of her mind, and inspired her efforts to revive him? Who can tell?

The former Signora's brother at Roccamonfina was rubbing his hands together with glee, and his obese wife, Donatella, was already packing in preparation for their removal from their current cramped quarters to the airy spaces of La Casa.

At the Black Toad the villagers were engrossed in dark deliberations on the evils of change. For all the Signor's original idiosyncrasies, and those oddities that were added to them following the first accident, all things considered he had been a good master to them over the years.

In the past when the Signora's brother visited, he had not created a good impression on the staff; he was a hypochondriac just as his sister had been, and he had a reputation for cruelty, depravity and avarice. The lady Donatella, known by her servants as the Beast of Roccamonfina, filled the hearts of the gathering with fear.

'Better the devil you know, my friends, than the devil you don't,' lisped Basilio Barile, from his baby chair, as Trofimo Barile, bursting with pride, knocked out his pipe in the grate. What a head that child had on his shoulders.

And what about Blandina? What would become of her under the new regime?

While her mother inhabited the sickroom, Blandina had been taking full advantage of her freedom with the young *signori*, and even the not so young ones. The approach to La Casa had been churned to mud by the volume of gentlemen beating a path to the door, and Semprebene Metrofano had been obliged to order a major scheme of works to replace the gravel and the grass verges.

With this newfound sophisticated company, Blandina was having the time of her life, and her former loves, Gordio Rossi, Gianluca Fuga and Lamberto Pedretti, were forced to look on as she behaved in a shameful way with her new admirers. Amongst the *signori* there were those who would stop at nothing to ingratiate themselves with the girl with a scent, without a heart. Brothers beat brothers. Cousins scrapped with uncles. Twins duelled to the death. It was rumoured that even the venerable Duc'd'Alba had come to blows with each of his seven sons over the favours of the fragrant filly.

CHAPTER FORTY-TWO

IN WHICH THE SIGNOR'S
EYES ARE OPENED

Many days of anxious waiting ensued, during which Ramona's eyes grew pinker after countless sleepless nights. She exhausted herself by her constant vigil at the bedside, yet she never gave a thought to her own depleted health. Her only concern was for her husband's survival, and with the utmost strength of her will she urged him to turn back from that dark place where he dwelt, and to return to life.

Dr Stipa infuriated his employer by appearing totally preoccupied, and indeed he was of no help at all in the sickroom. From the shaded windows he kept a constant watch on Blandina, and he was roused to the most bitter jealousy by what he saw.

Sometimes the Signor seemed actually to have departed, and a dark mantle fell over his face, on the livid canvas of which old scars fought with new for supremacy. At such times Ramona's eyes never left him, and her pink hand clutching at his grey one would try to transmit to it some of its own life force.

More than once did the lady Donatella and her entourage set out, forming the vanguard of the Roccamonfina faction. But these were false starts. When she had advanced no further than Teano, the lady would receive news that the old Signor had cheated death once more, and placing a curse upon him to speed his demise, she returned to the old home she was so impatient to leave.

What agonies of fear did Ramona feel as she nursed the Signor! Yet what she could not know was that his recovery following the first accident had taken exactly this path. At that time too there were endless vacillations: the minute advances towards survival, the minuscule retreats towards the vale of death.

Ramona prayed for his recovery with more feeling than she had ever prayed for anything in her life, and up in heaven San Andrea Corsini, invoked against sudden death, listened with a benevolent ear to her earnest entreaties. At long last, taking pity upon her, he decided to spare the life of her husband.

Yes, following the intercession of the saint, the Signor did finally rally. One day, when all hope seemed lost, he opened his lips and began to speak, responding, although still unconscious, to the voices that dwelt within his brain and aural passages.

'Right away, *generale*,' he said, and added, 'blow the bugle, deploy the first battalion.'

Although Ramona was not a lover of the voices that sometimes controlled her husband, on this occasion she was overjoyed to hear the

Signor speaking with them.

Thereafter the Signor made steady progress. His conversations with the voices grew more coherent. His eyes remained shut, but Ramona, stroking his gnarled hand, spoke to him in tender tones, and liked to believe he knew she was there with him. There was no way of predicting what the lasting effects of the accident would be, but he was now, Heaven be praised, out of danger.

The lady Donatella ventured forth no more, but left the goods wagons loaded just in case of a relapse, although her hope was at this stage beginning to fade. At the Black Toad there were celebrations as the servants had escaped her clutches, for a while at least.

Ramona had not spoken to Blandina since the accident, for which she considered her entirely responsible. But she would deal with her severely when the Signor recovered, of that the little minx could be sure.

One morning, after the Signor had passed a peaceful night, he was chattering away happily with the voices when the tranquil atmosphere of the sickroom was broken open by Blandina, bursting in and unleashing a ravishing cloud of scent that was more tantalizing and brazen than anything that could be imagined.

The huddle of medical experts who had joined the half-hearted Dr Stipa felt a surging in their loins that each was relieved to see replicated in his brethren, and, shockingly,

236

beneath the bedclothes of the patient.

'Leave the room,' hissed Ramona. 'You will disturb Papa.'

But it was too late, the Signor was already disturbed. The irresistible aroma had somehow prised open his nasal passages, and penetrated the spaghetti of his senses to reach his brain.

Immediately he opened his eyes and awoke from every delusion. His sense of smell was restored to him and he realized he had been played by the nose.

The odour he worshipped was not exuding from his wife after all. It was emanating from his nubile stepdaughter.

In that flash of enlightenment he knew the truth: he felt nothing for Ramona. Blandina was the object of his frenzied dreams, and the one desire of his heart.

EPILOGUE

Within the hour Ramona was expelled from La Casa with only the clothes she wore and a miniature reticule containing some crumpled banknotes, a sugared almond, and a few silver sequins.

The Signor, who had made a dramatic but defective recovery, was infuriated at the deceit he felt she had practised upon him. He had already written to his lawyers, instructing them to seek an annulment of the marriage, and was now able to apply himself wholeheartedly to the scent luxuriating within his restored nose.

Blandina was jubilant. From the top of the steps she laughed as she watched Ramona's retreat along the drive, and encouraged the crowd of seventeen *signori* gathered around her to take pot shots at her mother with their hunting guns. Fortunately for Ramona, they missed, but it was only because Blandina's aroma was causing the trigger fingers to tremble. Instead the Three Graces were peppered by shot, many windows were broken, and eleven of the under-gardeners were wounded. Once Ramona was out of sight, Blandina forgot her instantly and utterly, and flounced away to new amusements with her suitors.

Ramona was reeling, stunned by the speed

with which events had turned on her, and the ruthlessness with which the Signor had cast her out from his home and his heart. As she stumbled away from the estate, her blank mind not even considering what she should do next, she became aware of footsteps behind her on the lane. Turning, she saw it was Stiliano Mamiliano, red faced and puffing from the effort of running. His hair, although patchy, had started to grow back, and his ulcerated legs were gradually healing.

'Ramona Drottoveo,' he spluttered while still some way off. 'I mean, honoured Signora,' he continued, hastily correcting himself, 'I know I'm nothing but a lowly pig keeper, with a small thing and a bad smell, but I've always loved you . . .'